More Adventures
of the Great Brain

THE DIAL PRESS, INC.  NEW YORK

More Adventures
of the Great Brain

ILLUSTRATED BY MERCER MAYER

by John D. Fitzgerald

For Brynn

Contents

CHAPTER 1
The Night the Monster Walked 1

CHAPTER 2
The Taming of Britches Dotty 26

CHAPTER 3
The Time Papa Got Lost 61

CHAPTER 4
Tom Scoops Papa's Newspaper 81

CHAPTER 5
The Death of Old Butch 108

CHAPTER 6
The Ghost of Silverlode 119

More Adventures
of the Great Brain

The Night the Monster Walked

THERE WERE TWO GOOD REASONS for the people in Adenville to celebrate Christmas in 1896 besides the birth of Jesus Christ. It was the year that Utah became the forty-fifth state, and the year everybody in town believed my brother Tom had reformed. Papa went around with a happy look, believing he no longer had to worry about Tom making a fool out of him. Mamma was all smiles, believing no angry mother or father would be calling her on the telephone to complain my brother had swindled their son out of something. Aunt Bertha looked as if Tom had suddenly sprouted wings. Uncle Mark, who was the Marshal and Deputy Sheriff, thought all he had to deal with in the future would be law-breakers. It was the first Christmas parents bought presents for their sons, believing my brother wouldn't try to connive their kids out of them.

There was only one doubter in our midst, and that was my oldest brother, Sweyn, when he came home for the Christmas holidays from the Catholic Academy in Salt Lake City. Adenville only had a population of about twenty-five hundred people. About two thousand were Mormons, and the rest Catholics and Protestants. We had a one-room school-house, where Mr. Standish taught the first through the sixth grades. Any parents who wanted their children to get more education had to send them to Salt Lake City. There were plenty of places in Salt Lake City where the Mormons could send their kids for a higher education, because The Saints, as they preferred to be called, outnumbered other religions by ten to one. And there was more than one Academy for Protestants in the state capitol. But only one Catholic Academy.

Sweyn was thirteen. He was named after my Danish grandfather on my mother's side and had blonde hair like Mamma. I was now eight years old and would soon be nine. Tom was going on twelve. I had dark curly hair and brown eyes like Papa. Tom didn't look like Mamma exactly, and he didn't look like Papa. His hair wasn't blonde, and it wasn't dark. He was the only one in the family who had freckles.

"What has happened to the Great Brain?" Sweyn asked me two days after his arrival home, as we were stringing pop-corn to help decorate our Christmas tree. "He hasn't tried to connive me out of a single thing since I've been home."

"T.D. has reformed," I said. My brothers and I always called each other by the initials of our first and middle names, because that is how Papa addressed us. We all had the middle name of Dennis just like Papa, because it was a family tradition.

Sweyn held the darning needle threaded with string in one hand and a piece of popcorn in the other hand. He stared at me like I was plumb loco. "Bushwah!" he said. "That little conniver could no more reform than he could wash the freckles off his face."

I had never heard the word "bushwah" before and assumed it was a city slang word that Sweyn had picked up at the Academy. But I knew what it meant just from the way he said it.

I told him how Tom's great brain had helped Andy Anderson so he wasn't useless anymore with his peg leg. And how Tom had refused to accept the erector set he had been promised as payment if he helped Andy learn to do his chores and play—peg leg and all. And I told Sweyn how Tom had given me back my genuine Indian beaded belt, which he had swindled me out of earlier in the year.

"T.D. hasn't pulled a crooked stunt since," I concluded.

Sweyn thought about what I'd told him for a moment. "Once a conniver always a conniver," Sweyn said. "It doesn't sound like T.D. at all."

"Mr. and Mrs. Anderson both thanked Papa and Mamma for what Tom had done for their son," I said. "And I told them about him giving me back my belt."

Sweyn got a sly look on his face. "And what else did T.D. get you to tell Papa and Mamma?"

"Well," I said, "he did ask me to tell them he had his heart set on getting a bicycle for Christmas. He even got me to tell them the one he wanted at the Z.C.M.I. store." Zion's Cooperative Mercantile Institute was the full name of the town's big general store owned by the Mormon church. Some

3

people called it the Z.C.M.I. store, and some called it the Co-op.

"Ha, ha!" Sweyn exclaimed. "I knew it. T.D. with his cunning mind figured that a bicycle was worth more than an erector set or an old Indian beaded belt. This pretending to reform is all an act to get Papa and Mamma to give him a bike for Christmas."

Sure enough, Tom got his bike for Christmas. I got a new wagon. Sweyn got a pocket watch and watch fob. I guess it was about the happiest Christmas of my life, because it was the first time I didn't have to worry about Tom trying to swindle me out of my present.

Sweyn still had his doubts and put them into words just before he left to return to the Academy in Salt Lake City.

"I'll bet ten to one, J.D.," he said, "that the Great Brain resumes his career as a confidence man now that he has his bike."

My oldest brother was sure right. Tom started out the new year in his usual conniving style. It wouldn't have been so bad if it had been just one of his usual swindles. But this one got so complicated that armed men patrolled the streets of Adenville, and women and children had to remain behind locked doors.

Papa, who was editor and publisher of the *Adenville Weekly Advocate*, was considered the smartest man in town because he was the only one who had ever gone to college. Uncle Mark was considered one of the smartest peace officers in Utah. By the time Tom got through with his first scheme of the year, Papa was ready to admit he was the dumbest man in town except for Uncle Mark.

It all started our first day back at school during morning recess. A new kid in town named Parley Benson was showing

4

off a genuine Bowie knife his father had given him for Christmas. Parley was Tom's age, had yellow hair, and he always wore a coon-skin cap.

I knew Tom's great brain was working furiously to get that Bowie knife while he was riding me home on the handlebars of his new bike.

I was enjoying the ride as I looked at the trees planted by early Mormon pioneers that lined both sides of Main Street. Adenville was a typical small Mormon town but quite up to date. There were electric light poles all along Main Street, and we had telephones. There were wooden sidewalks in front of the stores. Straight ahead I could see the railroad tracks that separated the west side of town from the east side. Across the tracks on the east side were two saloons, the Sheepmen's Hotel, a rooming house, and some stores.

"That is some Bowie knife that new kid got for Christmas," Tom said.

I turned my head, and sure enough he had that old scheming look on his face.

"Sweyn was right," I said. "You only pretended to reform to get this bike for Christmas."

"You talk as though I were some kind of crook," Tom said, pretending I'd hurt his feelings. "Just because my great brain makes me smarter than any kid in town, and a lot of grownups, doesn't make me a crook. Papa always says that it's brains that count in this world."

"But Papa didn't say you are supposed to use your great brain to go around swindling people," I said.

"Who did I ever swindle?" Tom demanded.

"Me and every other kid in town," I said without a moment's hesitation.

5

"No two people can make a deal without both of them agreeing to it," he said. "Right?"

"Right," I said.

"And on all the deals we ever made, you agreed. Right, J.D.?"

I nodded my head.

"And no two people can make a bet without both of them believing they are going to win," he said. "Right?"

"Right again," I answered, wondering what he was leading up to.

"Then you've either got to admit that you are stupid and an easy mark or that I've never swindled you in my life," Tom said.

I sure as heck wasn't going to admit that I was stupid and an easy mark.

"I guess you are right," I said. "I'm sorry I called you a crook."

"But you did call me a crook," Tom said. "And when I tell Papa and Mamma that you called your own brother a crook, it will break their hearts."

"Please don't tell them," I pleaded.

"If I agree not to tell them," Tom said, "I think you should be punished for daring to call me a crook."

"I'll do anything you want," I said quickly.

Tom thought for a moment. "If you do my chores for a week, I just might not tell Papa and Mamma," he finally said.

"It's a deal," I said, and how I wished I'd learn to keep my big mouth shut. I knew if I told Papa and Mamma that Tom was a crook, it would break their hearts. But I also knew if I told them I was stupid and an easy mark, that would break their hearts too. The more I thought about it, the more grateful I was to Tom for letting me off so easy.

6

After we'd changed clothes, I filled up all the woodboxes in our kitchen, dining room, and parlor. Then I began bringing in buckets filled with coal from our coal and wood shed.

Mamma and Aunt Bertha were kneading biscuit dough for supper. Mamma tilted her head piled high with long golden braids and looked at me.

"Why are you doing your brother's chores?" she asked.

"It is all right, Mamma," I said, as I put down a heavy bucket filled with coal beside our big kitchen range. "I'm perfectly satisfied with the deal."

Aunt Bertha, who wasn't really our aunt but had lived with us so long she was just like one of the family, looked down at me from her great height as she brushed a strand of gray hair from her forehead with the back of her hand. She had hands and feet as big as a man's.

"Deal!" She said it as if it were a dirty word. "It was too good to be true. I knew it couldn't last. Tom is at it again."

Mamma looked concerned. "Is Tom D. taking advantage of you?" she asked.

"No, Mamma," I said, because I thought Tom had let me off easy.

Tom sat on the corral fence while I fed and watered the chickens, milk cow, team of horses, and Sweyn's mustang, Dusty. I was exhausted when I joined Tom on the corral fence.

"That new kid Parley Benson sure likes to brag," Tom said.

"You mean how he bragged about his father being an animal bounty hunter for the ranchers?" I asked.

"Yes," Tom answered. "And how brave his father is, and how brave he is."

"I guess it does take a lot of courage to track down and kill mountain lions, wolves, coyotes, and other animals that kill livestock," I said.

"Sure it does, but that doesn't make Parley brave like his father," Tom said. "If there is anything I can't stand, it is a kid who boasts."

I knew if Tom couldn't stand it, he was going to put a stop to it. "Are you going to put your great brain to work to cure Parley of his bragging?" I asked. I couldn't help feel excited.

Tom grinned. "And teach him a lesson at the same time," he said.

"I'd hate to be in his shoes," I said.

On the first Saturday after school had started in the new year, it was snowing in the mountains and raining in town. Tom went up to his loft in the barn to put his great brain to work on how to cure Parley Benson from bragging while I did all the chores.

It continued to rain after we'd eaten lunch. We went to the barn to wait for our friends, who always came there to play when the weather was bad. Tom and I were sitting on a bale of hay when Basil Kokovinis entered. He was a Greek boy, whose father owned the Palace Cafe. He was Tom's age and had big dark eyes and black hair.

"It's a pour down," Basil said as he took off his cap and yellow rain slicker.

"Downpour," Tom corrected Basil, who had trouble with the English language since he had been in this country less than a year.

Danny Forester, Sammy Leeds, and Parley Benson were the next to arrive. Parley and Danny were Tom's age and

Sammy one year older. Sammy had what Sweyn called a city-slicker look. I'd never seen a city slicker, but assumed my brother meant Sammy always had a sly, know-it-all look on his face. Danny's left eyelid was half closed like it was most of the time—as if one half of him wanted to go to sleep and the other half to stay awake. Parley was wearing his coon-skin cap and had his Bowie knife in a scabbard on his belt.

Then Howard Kay and Jimmie Peterson, who were my age, came into the barn with rain dripping from their caps and slickers. Howard had a round face like a Halloween pumpkin. Jimmie's mother always bought his clothes a size too large so they would last for two years, because she had no younger sons to wear Jimmie's hand-me-downs. This was the year Jimmie's clothes were too big for him and hung on him like a scarecrow's.

"What are we going to play?" Sammy asked.

"How about follow-the-leader?" Tom suggested. Then he looked at Parley. "And since Parley has been bragging all week about how brave he is, let's make him the leader."

"I can do things none of you kids can do," Parley boasted, as he removed the Bowie knife from his scabbard and laid it on a bale of hay.

It didn't take me long to believe it. Parley climbed up the rope ladder to Tom's loft with us following. He went hand-over-hand across the rafters to the other side of the barn. We could all follow him. But on the way back Parley swung himself and only grabbed every other rafter. Howard, Jimmie, and I had to drop out. Then Parley went hand-over-hand to a rafter. I stood bug-eyed as he hung by his toes from the rafter. Then he let go with his toes, and I was sure he'd dash his brains out on the floor of the barn. But he turned a flip-flop in mid air and landed on his feet. That was the end of playing

9

follow-the-leader because not even Tom or Basil could do a stunt like that.

Sammy patted Parley on the back. "What a stunt," he said. "I guess that makes you the bravest kid in town all right."

"I wouldn't say that," Tom said. "Would you say the circus acrobats are the bravest people in the world? What takes real courage is to do something nobody else has ever done. I know if Basil and I practice, we can learn to do that stunt. What takes real courage is an explorer going into a wild and strange country where no man has ever been."

"My Pa goes places no man has ever been," Parley boasted.

"We were talking about you and not your father," Tom said. "Now if a boy had the courage to go someplace like the entrance chamber of Skeleton Cave at night, knowing there are monsters and big snakes in the cave, that would take real courage."

"Baloney," Sammy said. "Frank and Allan Jensen were lost in the cave before you and your Uncle Mark rescued them. If there are real monsters and big snakes in the cave, why didn't they attack you?"

"The only thing that saved us all from the monsters and big snakes," Tom said with a serious look on his face, "was that the Jensen brothers had their dog Lady with them, and Uncle Mark and I had J.D.'s dog Brownie with us. I saw plenty of monsters, but they had never seen a dog or heard a dog bark, and they were afraid. I'm talking about going to the cave without any dog to scare away the monsters."

Parley patted the Bowie knife in his scabbard. "I'll bet I wouldn't be afraid with my Bowie knife," he said.

Tom picked a straw from a bale of hay and put it in his

mouth. "I wasn't thinking of betting," he said as the straw wiggled up and down. "But now that you mention it, I'll bet that you are afraid to meet me in the entrance chamber of Skeleton Cave next Saturday night after curfew."

"Why not tonight?" Parley asked.

"You are new in town," Tom said. "I want to be fair and give you a chance to find out all you can about the cave."

"It's a bet," Parley said.

"But we haven't bet anything yet," Tom said. "I'll tell you what I'll do. I'll bet my air rifle, my jackknife, and twenty-five cents in cash against your Bowie knife that you are afraid to meet me." Then Tom shrugged. "If we both show up, the bet is off."

"It's a bet," Parley said quickly. "I know I'll be there."

The next morning I finished my last morning of doing all Tom's chores and my own chores just in time to help Papa and Tom freeze the ice cream for our Sunday dinner.

Tom's great brain worked like sixty that day. When he came down from his loft about an hour after dinner, he had a big grin on his face.

"Your great brain did it!" I shouted as he came out of the barn and into our corral, where I'd been standing guard to see he wasn't disturbed.

Tom nodded. "I'm going to convince Parley Benson there are monsters in the cave," he said. "That will make him afraid to meet me there."

"How?" I asked, curious as all get out.

Tom ignored my question by asking one. "Have you ever seen the footprint of a monster?"

"No," I answered.

12

"Has anybody in town ever seen the footprint of a monster?" Tom asked.

"I don't see how,' 'I said.

"Then nobody knows what the footprint of a monster looks like," Tom said with a grin. "I'm going to make footprints of a monster. Give me your word you won't say anything to Papa or Mama or anybody, and I'll let you help."

I sure didn't want to be left out. "I give my word," I promised.

"We'll saddle up Dusty first," Tom said. "If we meet any kids, just tell them we are going for a ride."

After we'd put the saddle and bridle on Dusty, I watched Tom pick up a gunny sack. He mounted the mustang and rode out of the corral, waiting for me to shut the gate. Then he helped me up behind him. Tom guided the mustang up and down alleys and in a roundabout way until we were in back of the slaughterhouse by the stockyards. The odor was terrible because there were piles of old steer hooves, hides, bones, and skulls.

Tom got off Dusty with the gunny sack. He went to the pile of hooves and picked out three split-toed ones, which he put in the gunny sack.

He didn't say a word until we were back in the barn and had put Dusty back in his stall.

"Go to the toolshed and get the saw, a hammer, and some horseshoe nails," he ordered me.

When I returned, Tom held the hooves on a bale of hay and sawed off the bone on top so they would be level. He told me to get a shovel and bury the pieces of bone behind the barn.

When I came back, he had a piece of board which was to have been used for kindling wood. He sawed off two pieces about one foot square. Then he got an old belt of Papa's from his loft and cut off two pieces of leather about six inches long.

"Now J.D.," he said to me "you go outside and stand guard. Don't let anybody in the barn."

I was curious as anything but did as I was told. I stood outside the barn door, where I could hear Tom hammering inside the barn. Finally he called me to come inside.

"Shut the door and stand with your back against it," he said.

Then he held up the two pieces of board so I could see what he'd done. He'd nailed three of the halves of the steers' hooves to the bottom of each board with the toes all pointing in different directions. Then he put the boards on the ground, and I could see he'd nailed a strap across the top of each board. I stood bug-eyed as Tom stuck the toes of his shoes under the straps. He then walked a few steps and turned around.

"Behold the footprints of a monster!" he said.

I looked at the footprints he'd made in the dirt. They looked like the tracks of a huge three-toed animal.

Tom began rubbing his hands together. "When I get through, Parley and the other kids will swear there are monsters in Skeleton Cave."

Tom took the gunny sack and erased the footprints in the dirt. Then he said triumphantly, "That Bowie knife is as good as mine right now. I'll sneak out after curfew Friday night and make footprints from Skeleton Cave down to the river and back. Saturday morning all I've got to do is to get Parley and the other kids down by the river so they can see the tracks. If Parley thinks there are monsters in that cave, he'll never meet me Saturday night."

14

"Why would the monster come out of the cave?" I asked.

"I'll make them think the monster came down to the river to get a drink of water," Tom answered.

I shivered. "Maybe there are real monsters in the cave," I said.

"I sure didn't see any," Tom said. "All Uncle Mark and I saw were a lot of bats."

"What if Frank and Allan Jensen tell Parley there are nothing but bats in the cave?" I asked, only wanting to help.

"I'm going to take care of that right now," Tom said. "I'm going to remind them I saved their lives, and they owe me a favor. I never told you this before, J.D., but Uncle Mark made Frank and Allan and me promise we'd say we'd seen monsters and giant snakes in the cave."

"Why would he do that?" I asked.

"To scare any kids from ever going exploring in the cave again," Tom answered.

"You never told me that," I said, feeling cheated.

"Would I lie to my own brother?" Tom asked.

The next morning during recess I saw Parley Benson talking to Frank and Allan Jensen. They sure must have laid it on thick because Parley looked positively pale.

I thought Friday would never come, but it finally did. I locked my dog Brownie and the pup up in the barn after supper. When it was bedtime, I got undressed, but Tom kept his clothes on. He waited until the curfew whistle blew and then climbed out our bedroom window and shinnied down the elm tree. I was determined to stay awake, but the next thing I knew it was morning. Tom was still asleep. I woke him up.

"How did it go?" I asked all excited.

"Perfect," he answered. "I went all the way to the small

15

inner chamber of the cave and made footprints down to the river and all the way back. Then I took off the footprints and carried them and erased my own footprints inside both chambers. When Parley sees those footprints, it will cure him of his bragging and cost him his Bowie knife."

I was just finishing my first stack of buckwheat cakes with melted butter and maple sugar when Uncle Mark came into our kitchen. He was usually calm like a peace officer should be, but this morning he looked all excited.

"Pete Jorgenson came to my house this morning just as we were finishing breakfast," he said to Papa. "He told me he'd seen some strange tracks leading from Skeleton Cave down to the river. I went to investigate. You won't believe this, but there are tracks of an animal I've never seen leading from the cave to the river and back."

"What kind of tracks?" Papa asked while he wiped his mouth with his napkin.

"They are the footprints of an animal of some kind. They have a three-pronged hoof with three toes pointing in different directions," Uncle Mark replied.

Papa jumped to his feet. "A prehistoric animal that has made its home in the cave all these years!" he shouted. "What a news story this will make!"

Mamma didn't share Papa's enthusiasm. "You said you saw underground rivers in the cave when the Jensen boys got lost," she said to Uncle Mark. "Why would any such animal come down to the river to drink?"

"For any one of half a dozen reasons," Papa exclaimed. "Underground rivers run dry. The animal could have got lost in the miles of underground caverns and labyrinths in the cave and found its way to the entrance in search of water."

"I think the best thing to do," Uncle Mark said, "is to

get the Mayor's permission and dynamite the entrance to the cave so the beast can't get out again. I've been wanting to seal up that cave ever since the Jensen boys got lost in it."

"You'll do no such thing," Papa said. "Think of what this means to science. If the animal came out once to drink, it will come out again. I'll send a telegram right off to the Smithsonian Institution asking them to send an expert on pre-historic animals to Adenville."

Papa was so excited he ran out of the house with his napkin still tied around his neck.

"Keep the boys in the house," Uncle Mark said to Mamma. Then he ran after Papa.

Aunt Bertha raised her big arms over her head. "A live monster in our midst!" she cried out. "The Lord preserve us!"

Tom excused himself from the table without finishing his breakfast.

"Where do you think you are going?" Mamma demanded.

"I've got to see Papa," Tom answered.

"You and John D. will do exactly as your Uncle Mark said. You won't step a foot out of this house," Mamma said. "This animal or beast or whatever it is could be very dangerous."

"But there is something I've got to tell Papa," Tom said. "I'll telephone him at the *Advocate*."

"You will not," Mamma said. "Your Uncle Mark is going to have the switchboard tied up letting everybody in town know they shouldn't let anyone out of their homes. Whatever it is you want to tell your father can wait."

Tom and I went up to our room. "Who would believe grownups could be such fools?" he asked, plenty disgusted. "I figured Parley and the kids might swallow the story, but how could intelligent men like Papa and Uncle Mark believe such an impossible thing?"

"You'd better figure out some way to tell Papa those footprints are a fake," I said.

Tom thought for a moment, and then he smiled. "Papa will know they are fake when he sees them," he said confidently. "Papa is a college graduate, and they must have taught him all about prehistoric animals in college."

My brother couldn't have been more wrong. Uncle Mark swung into action first by telephoning everybody in town to lock their doors and keep all women and children inside. He swore in fifty deputies to patrol the streets armed with rifles and shotguns. The whole town became paralyzed with terror to the point of panic. Many families decided it was a good time to visit relatives outside Adenville.

Papa telephoned he wouldn't be home for lunch. By suppertime Tom had decided things had gone this far, he might as well wait until morning to tell Papa, so he could collect his bet from Parley. Anyway the damage had already been done. Papa told us during supper that he'd sent telegrams to the Salt Lake City newspapers and got out an Extra of the *Advocate*. Uncle Mark had posted lookouts and promised if the monster came to the river to drink that night, he would send for Papa.

When Tom and I went to bed, my brother insisted he was going through with his plan. When the curfew whistle blew, he took the screen off our bedroom window and shinnied down the elm tree.

It wasn't until Tom disappeared into the darkness that I became afraid. I knew he had made the footprints, but that was no guarantee there weren't monsters and giant snakes in the cave. There were plenty of grownups who believed there

18

were. I kept getting more frightened until I was shaking all over. Maybe it was true the big snakes and monsters had been frightened of Lady and Brownie. But Lady was home, and Brownie was locked up in the barn. One of those giant snakes or big monsters was just lying in wait for my brother and would gobble him up. I'd never see Tom again. My fear gave way to panic. I jumped out of bed and ran downstairs into the parlor. Papa was talking to Uncle Mark.

"T.D. has gone to Skeleton Cave!" I screamed.

"Now why would he do that?" Papa asked testily. Papa was always one to take a second thought, and when it came, he jumped to his feet. "Good Lord!" he shouted.

Mamma and Aunt Bertha came running into the parlor from the kitchen, where they had been making sandwiches and coffee for the men on patrol.

"Patrol the streets!" Papa shouted at Uncle Mark.

"The streets are patrolled," Uncle Mark said. "I wish they weren't now. In all the excitement some trigger-happy deputy might take a shot at the boy."

Papa and Uncle Mark dashed out of the house before I could tell them the footprints were a fake.

"What in the world has got into your father and uncle?" Mamma asked.

"T.D. sneaked out after curfew and went to Skeleton Cave!" I cried.

"Oh dear God," Mamma cried. Then she knelt on the floor and began to pray.

I don't know how long we remained there until Aunt Bertha broke the silence.

"Why in the name of heaven would the boy do such a thing?" she asked helplessly.

"It isn't what Tom D. has done that counts," Mamma

19

said. "The only thing that matters is that they return my son to me safely."

It seemed like a long time before our parlor door opened, and in came Papa and Uncle Mark and my brother. Papa waited until Mamma and Aunt Bertha had made a fuss over Tom and assured themselves he was all right. Then he folded his arms on his chest.

"And now T.D.," he said sternly, "it will be most interesting to hear why you risked being shot by a nervous deputy or being killed by a prehistoric monster, and almost gave all of us heart failure in the bargain."

"I made a bet with Parley Benson," Tom said as if he went around scaring the daylights out of people every day in the week. "You and Uncle Mark are my witnesses that I was in the entrance to Skeleton Cave tonight after curfew, and Parley wasn't there."

Papa unfolded his arms and clasped his hands to the side of his head. He sort of staggered to his rocking chair and slumped down in it.

"Oh no!" he cried out as if he had a sudden pain in his stomach.

Uncle Mark looked steadily at Tom. "What kind of bet?" he asked.

"I bet Parley my air rifle, jackknife, and twenty-five cents in cash against his Bowie knife that he would be afraid to meet me in Skeleton Cave tonight," Tom answered. "My great brain figured out a way to cure Parley of his bragging and teach him a lesson at the same time."

Then Uncle Mark spoke sharply to my brother. "Do you realize that you could have been shot and killed by one of my deputies?"

20

Tom smiled confidently. "I knew with my great brain I could sneak past your patrols easily," he said.

"And you still went there knowing this beast or whatever it is might have killed you?" Uncle Mark asked.

Tom looked at Papa. "About those tracks, Papa," he said.

I couldn't remain quiet any longer. "T.D.'s great brain figured out how to win the bet from Parley," I said. "I helped him get the hooves from behind the slaughterhouse and stood guard outside the barn while he made the footprints of the monster."

"I think," Mamma said severely, "that Tom Dennis had better do his own explaining."

"I sneaked out after curfew last night," Tom confessed, "and made the tracks from the cave down to the river and back. I knew if Parley thought there was a real live monster in that cave, he wouldn't go near it tonight. And I'd win the bet." He tapped his temple with his finger. "Some brain, huh, Mamma."

"I should have known," Uncle Mark said slowly. "The tracks weren't deep enough to have been made by anything as heavy as a prehistoric animal." He looked helplessly around the room. "This will make me the laughingstock of every peace officer in Utah," he said in a very tired voice.

"Make *you* a laughingstock!" Papa exclaimed, flapping his arms as if he were trying to fly. "My reputation as a journalist is ruined. I'm finished."

"I was going to tell you the footprints were fake," Tom protested, "but Mamma wouldn't let me."

Papa looked at Mamma as if she'd just stabbed him in the back. "I can't believe that you, of all people, would help to perpetrate such a cruel joke," he said.

"I knew nothing about the fake footprints," Mamma

21

said. "Tom D. did mention he had something to tell you this morning, but I didn't think it was important and told him it could wait."

Tom nodded. "And when you came home for supper, it was too late," he said. "I figured the damage was done, so I might as well win my bet."

Uncle Mark sure looked mighty glum. "I don't know what I'll do, or where we will go after I turn my badge in," he said.

"I was only trying to scare Parley away from the cave," Tom said, trying to defend himself. "I thought he and the other kids might believe there was a live monster in the cave, but I never in a million years thought that grownups would believe such an impossible thing."

To my surprise Mamma began to smile. "I guess that puts you both in your place," she said, apparently getting even for what Papa had said to her.

"Don't worry, Papa," Tom said. "My great brain can save both you and Uncle Mark. I put it to work this morning right after Mamma wouldn't let me go tell you about the tracks. All you've got to do is to seal up the entrance to the cave by dynamiting it, and nobody will ever be able to prove there wasn't a live monster."

A smile tugged at the corner of Uncle Mark's lips. "I know the Mayor will give his permission, because people have been asking him to seal up the cave entrance since the Jensen brothers got lost in it. That leaves just the tracks."

Papa appeared to suddenly decide he wanted to live on this earth a little longer. "Pierre Dussierre has a herd of sheep in the stockyards," he said. "I'll get him to drive that herd from the river up to the cave and leave them grazing on Cedar Ridge as soon as you seal up the entrance."

22

Then Papa looked at Tom, and his face wasn't fatherly at all, but downright unfriendly. "You boys go to bed," he commanded. "I'll deal with you in the morning."

Tom and I were sound asleep when a mighty blast of dynamite shook our house.

The next morning a herd of sheep was grazing on Cedar Ridge, and you couldn't have found a trace of the fake footprints with a magnifying glass.

I thought for sure that Tom's brilliant idea would make the punishment light, but it didn't. Papa handed down his sentence right after we'd finished eating breakfast.

"A person who cheats to win a bet is no better than a person who steals," Papa said to Tom. "You will call off your bet with Parley Benson. And you will give me your word of honor that you will never make another bet with another boy."

Tom's face took on the look of a boy who has just lost a beaut of a Bowie knife. "I promise, word of honor," he said reluctantly. "But don't forget, Papa, that you and Uncle Mark cheated by letting people believe there really was a monster."

Papa took a deep breath, which he held so long his cheeks puffed up, and his face turned red. Then he slowly exhaled.

"You are right," he admitted, "but only about the footprints and the monster story. Sneaking out of the house after curfew for two straight nights is an entirely different matter. And for that, T.D., you will not receive your allowance for doing your chores for the next four weeks. And because J.D. conspired with you I hereby pronounce a sentence of one week of the silent treatment on both of you."

Tom and I were the most unfortunate kids in town.

When any other kids did something wrong, all they got was a whipping. When Tom and I did something wrong, we got the silent treatment, which was ten times worse than a whipping. It meant that Papa and Mamma wouldn't speak to us, and if we spoke to them, they would pretend they didn't hear us. It was as if Tom and I didn't exist as far as they were concerned during the silent treatment. How I wished they would act like normal parents and give us a whipping, and get it all over with in a hurry.

Papa sent a telegram to the Smithsonian Institution, informing them it was all a hoax. Star reporters from Salt Lake City and Denver and even one from San Francisco came to Adenville but were unable to prove the story of the night the monster walked was a hoax. After all, hundreds of people had seen the tracks of the monster, and Uncle Mark said he'd sealed up the entrance to the cave to protect the lives of the citizens of Adenville. None of the newspapermen seemed interested in opening the cave and searching for the monster. And Pierre Dussierre said he hadn't even heard about the tracks of the monster when he put his herd of sheep out to graze on Cedar Ridge.

My little brain couldn't figure out how the minds of grownups worked. Tom had saved Papa's reputation as an editor and publisher and saved Uncle Mark's reputation as a Marshal and Deputy Sheriff. I thought he should be entitled to a reward instead of being punished. But my little brain did figure out something about telling a lie. A kid tells a lie and his parents give him a whipping or punishment of some kind. But his parents can tell lies all over the place, like Papa did, and that is all right, because they are grownups. The way I figured it was that when our parents were kids, they got punished for telling lies. The only way they could get even was to wait until they had kids of their own to punish for telling lies. Well, I'd show Papa and Mamma. Boy, oh boy, when I'm grown up, I'll be the biggest liar in the world, and I'll hand down sentences of a whole month's silent treatment on my own kids every time they lie.

CHAPTER TWO

The Taming of Britches Dotty

ON MONDAY MORNING AFTER the Saturday that
Tom had terrorized the town, Mr. Standish asked him to take
the midterm examination with the sixth graders instead of
the fifth graders. He said if Tom passed the examination that
he would promote my brother to the sixth grade, so Tom
could graduate in June. Mr. Standish always let superior pupils skip a grade if they could pass the midterm examination
for the next grade. It was no trick at all for Tom to get an *A*.
So he moved from his desk in the fifth row with the fifth
graders to the last row with the sixth graders.

A couple of weeks later when Papa came home from the
Advocate office, he had something on his mind. He told

Mamma he had let a man named Charles Blake and his daughter move into the old adobe house. Papa and Mamma had lived there when they first got married. It was furnished with our old furniture and had a small and large bedroom, a parlor, and a big kitchen. Papa put off telling Mamma about it until we had finished eating supper.

"Blake?" Mamma asked as she rolled up her napkin and placed it in her silver napkin ring. "I don't recall anybody by that name in town. How much rent is he going to pay?"

Papa sort of coughed like something was stuck in his throat. "You know, Tena, that house has been vacant since the Palmers moved to Cedar City," Papa said. "A house lasts longer when people are living in it."

"I see," Mamma said. "You told Mr. Blake he could live in the house rent-free. But why?"

"He isn't a Mormon for one thing," Papa answered. "You know how the Mormons look out for their own. If he were a Mormon, they would see to it that Blake and his daughter had a place to live and find some kind of work for the man."

"Just who is he?" Mamma asked.

"He was a wrangler who caught wild horses and broke them to the saddle or harness and sold them to ranchers," Papa answered. "He owned a small spread over near the Nevada line. A few months ago a wild horse fell on him and broke his leg in several places and also permanently injured his back so he can never ride again. What little money he had was soon gone, and he lost his small ranch."

Mamma shook her head. "The poor man," she said sadly.

"Dave Ecord gave Blake and the daughter a ride into town," Papa continued. "He dropped them off at the *Advocate* office this afternoon, thinking I might help the man find some kind of work in town. Blake's injuries make it impossible for him to do any heavy work, and he can't work standing up because he has to use a crutch to get around."

"What kind of work could he possibly do?" Mamma asked.

"That part I took care of this afternoon," Papa said. "I remembered Jerry Stout telling me a few weeks ago that he was getting older and had more business than he could handle. I took Blake to see Jerry. Jerry offered to give Blake a job and teach him how to repair saddles, harnesses, and bridles in his shop. It is work that can be done sitting down. And Blake doesn't know it, but Jerry told me that if things work out, he will sell the shop to him when he retires in a few years."

"That was very nice of Jerry," Mamma said.

Papa's face became solemn. "Getting Blake settled was easy," he said. "The daughter is much more of a problem. Blake lost his wife several years ago. Since that time, he has taken the girl with him into the mountains and plains to capture wild horses. He's raised her like a boy. She is about twelve years old and has never attended school. I just don't see how she will be able to adjust to life in town. It will be like a prison to her. She is like a wild creature. Her father calls her Dotty."

"All she needs is love and help," Mamma said.

"It is going to take more than that," Papa insisted. "I doubt if she has ever worn a dress in her life. She wears Levi britches, a boy's shirt, and boy's cowboy boots."

"That is no problem," Mamma said. "I know several mothers who have clothing their daughters have outgrown. And Bertha and I can make the girl some dresses and things."

"In my judgment," Papa said soberly, "she wouldn't accept them or wear them, and her father wouldn't permit it

28

anyway. They are a proud and stubborn pair. Blake insisted I make out a promissory note for him to sign with an X, promising to pay me rent when he gets on his feet, before he'd move into the adobe house."

Mamma stared at Papa. "Mr. Blake can't read or write?" she asked.

"Ignorant but proud," Papa said.

The next morning after we'd finished our morning chores, Mamma called Tom and me into the kitchen. She pointed at a bushel basket on the table. It was lined with wrapping paper. I could see a smoked ham, fruit jars, and several jars of homemade jellies and jams.

"You boys take this to the Blakes," she said.

Tom and I grabbed hold of the wire handles and carried the basket down Main Street to Third Street South, where we turned left. The adobe house was in the middle of the block. As we got near it, we stopped and stared.

There was a girl wearing Levi britches, a boy's shirt, and short cowboy boots washing a window with her back turned toward us. I wouldn't have known it was a girl, if it hadn't been for her yellow hair tied in a braid behind her back.

We continued on and set the basket on the small front porch of the adobe house.

The girl heard us and turned around. She had a round face burned a deep brown from outdoor living. Her face looked like it had been dunked in a barrel of freckles. She stared at us with unfriendly blue eyes.

"I'm Tom Fitzgerald, and this is my brother John," Tom introduced us. "You must be Dotty Blake. Our mother and family welcome you and your father to Adenville and have sent you a few things."

29

I thought it was a very neighborly and nice speech myself, but Dotty's eyes flashed.

"Us Blakes don't take charity from nobody," she said. At least she sounded like a girl when she talked.

"It isn't charity," Tom said. "It is just being neighborly."

"Ain't no difference," she said. "Take it back. Me and Pa don't need help from nobody."

Tom shrugged as he looked at me. We picked up the bushel basket and carried it back home. We told Mamma what had happened, after setting the basket on the kitchen floor.

Mamma shook her head sadly. "I guess your father was right," she said.

The next morning we went to the Community Church as usual, because there was no Catholic Church in Adenville. A Catholic missionary priest came to town about once a year to baptize Catholic babies, marry Catholics, and hold confessions and Masses for a few days in the Community Church. Papa said going to hear the Reverend Holcomb preach at the Community Church was better than no church at all. Mr. Blake was there dressed in overalls and a blue work shirt, I guess because he didn't own a suit. And Dotty was there bold as brass in her Levi britches, boy's shirt, and cowboy boots. Reverend Holcomb didn't seem to mind and welcomed them to the congregation.

"I'm going to call on the Blakes," Mamma said when we returned home.

"Do you think that's wise?" Papa asked. "Mr. Blake and his daughter have given every indication all they want is to be left alone."

"I have every right to see how they are taking care of our house," Mamma said. "I'll use that as an excuse. Then I'll try to reason with Mr. Blake that being neighborly isn't charity."

This was too exciting to miss, so Tom and I waited in our parlor with Papa and Aunt Bertha until Mamma returned. She sure looked worried and sad as she sat down in her maple rocker.

"That girl has the house as neat as a pin," she said.

"Then what are you worried about?" Papa asked.

"It isn't the house," Mamma said. "It's that poor girl and her stubborn father. He lets her do the housework and cooking but otherwise treats her like a son and not a daughter. He even boasted to me how he had raised her as if she were a boy, and how she could ride, use a lariat, a rifle, and other things better than a boy. I first tried to reason with him, pointing out that now they were living in town, and he should treat her as a daughter and not as a son. And do you know what he said?"

Papa waited as Mamma paused and then asked, "How could I know? I wasn't there."

Mamma shook her head. "He said he liked his daughter just the way she was, and it was nobody else's business how he raised her. Then I pointed out to him that living in town did have some advantages, such as enabling his daughter to get an education. And do you know what he said to that?"

Papa was getting impatient with Mamma as she paused again. "My dear Tena, how could I possibly know?"

"He said he didn't hold with book learning," Mamma said. "The man is impossible."

I was one hundred percent in favor of Mr. Blake. Any father who didn't want his kid to go to school was all right for my money.

"There is nothing we can do about it," Papa said. "It is Mr. Blake's business how he raises his daughter."

31

Mamma stood up with that look of determination on her face I'd seen so many times. "I am going to make it my business, and you are going to help me. We are going to force Mr. Blake to make his daughter go to school."

"How?" Papa asked.

"You will go see Calvin Whitlock and other members of the school board this afternoon and convince them it is to the best interests of Dotty Blake that she get an education," Mamma said.

When Papa returned home late that afternoon, he seemed in good spirits.

"Well?" Mamma asked.

"It is all set," Papa said. "Calvin and the members of the school board, along with Mark representing the law, will call on Mr. Blake in the morning. They will tell him the law forces all children to attend school through the sixth grade. Blake can't read, so there is no way for him to look up the law. Jerry Stout and others Blake might ask about it have all agreed to cooperate."

The next morning Mr. Whitlock entered our one-room schoolhouse looking very distinguished with his gray, muttonchop side whiskers. He was accompanied by Dotty Blake and her father. Mr. Blake had yellow hair and a yellow mustache. His face was burned as brown as an Indian's skin. He was hobbling on a homemade crutch.

"This is Dorthea Blake," Mr. Whitlock said to Mr. Standish. "She has never been to school. You will have to start her in the first grade, and be patient with her."

Then Mr. Whitlock and Mr. Blake left. Dotty looked scared and was biting her lower lip. She was wearing her Levi britches, boy's shirt, and cowboy boots. Our teacher showed her to a seat in the front row with the first graders.

32

"Welcome to our school, Dorthea," Mr. Standish said.

"My name's Dotty and not Dorthea," she said.

"Mr. Whitlock said your name was Dorthea, and that is what you will be called in school," Mr. Standish said with authority.

"Guess my pa knows my name better'n Mr. Whitlock," Dotty said. "Pa calls me Dotty."

Mr. Standish sort of shrugged. "All right, Dotty, if that is the way you prefer it," he said.

Mr. Standish tried to include Dotty in the lessons for the first grade, but she just sat with her arms folded and wouldn't answer him.

When our teacher finally released us for the morning recess, Tom whispered to me, "That poor kid is in for a rough time."

Tom was right. No sooner had the kids got outside on the playground when they began making fun of Dotty. Sammy Leeds was the ringleader.

"Are you a boy or a girl?" Sammy asked as all the kids crowded around her. "Can't tell with those britches, boy's shirt, and boots you're wearing."

Then Marie Vinson put in her two cents. "Britches Dotty hasn't got a dress to wear," she shouted and then laughed.

Christine Mackie kept the insults going. "Why didn't your mother wash and curl your hair?" she asked.

"Ain't got no ma," Dotty said. "She's dead."

I thought that would make the kids ashamed, but it didn't.

Sammy laughed a cruel laugh. "Britches Dotty can't read or write," he shouted. "Britches Dotty is dumb, dumb, dumb."

Then all the kids except Tom and me and Basil began to

33

shout: "Britches Dotty is dumb, dumb, dumb!" Sammy was the worst of all, stepping right up close to her and shouting the insult right in her face. She pushed him away.

"You stop makin' fun of me, or you'll be sorry," she said with a wild look in her blue eyes.

"Sorry about what?" Sammy taunted her.

"About this!" Dotty shouted, as she hauled off and punched Sammy right on the nose so hard it began to bleed.

All the girls began insulting Sammy, because they had never seen a girl fight a boy.

Marie Vinson shouted, "Sammy got a bloody nose from a girl!"

As if by signal, all the girls began to shout, "Sammy got whipped by a girl! Sammy got whipped by a girl!"

Sammy wiped the blood from his nose with his handkerchief. He looked angry enough to explode. "If you wasn't a girl, I'd beat the tar out of you," he said through gritted teeth.

"I ain't afraid to fight you," Dotty said.

That was all Sammy needed. He doubled up his fists and began throwing punches at Dotty, who fought just like a boy and punched him right back.

The kids began to scream and shout. This brought Mr. Standish out of the schoolhouse. Tom ran to meet the teacher with me following.

"Please let them fight," Tom pleaded. "If Dotty whips Sammy, all the other kids will leave her alone."

Mr. Standish thought about it for a moment and then went back into the schoolhouse.

By the time Tom and I got back to the fight, Sammy and Dotty were in a clinch. I watched bug-eyed as Dotty wrestled Sammy to the ground and pinned him with her knees on his arms. She pasted him good a few times on the face. Then she scooped up a handful of dirt.

"Had 'nuff?" she asked.

Poor old Sammy knew he was beat. "I give up," he said.

"Then eat dirt," Dotty shouted, as she pushed the handful of dirt into Sammy's mouth.

It was one of the worst humiliations a fellow could suffer. Sammy began to gag and spit dirt and blood from his mouth as Dotty got up. And boy, did she have a wild look as she stared at the kids.

"The next one who makes fun of me, I'll fight and make eat dirt—boy or girl," she threatened.

All the kids backed away from Dotty with scared looks. Just then Mr. Standish rang the bell ending recess.

Dotty's first day in school must have been enough to make Mr. Standish wish he'd never become a teacher. He tried several times to get Dotty learning her *ABC's*, but she just sat with her arms folded and wouldn't say a word.

"Wouldn't you like to learn to read and write like the other pupils?" he asked.

"Nope," Dotty answered, speaking for the first time that afternoon.

"Wouldn't you like to learn something about the history of our great country?" Mr. Standish asked.

"Nope," Dotty said.

"Wouldn't you like to learn how to add and subtract and multiply figures?" Mr. Standish asked.

"Nope," Dotty said. "My pa told me I gotta come here 'cause it's the law, but he didn't say I gotta learn anything."

Mr. Standish threw up his hands. "Is there anything you do like?" he asked.

"Horses," Dotty said. "I like horses."

35

That evening after supper Tom and I did our homework on the dining-room table and then went into the parlor to play a game or two of dominoes before going to bed.

Papa laid aside his book. "How did Dotty Blake's first day in school go?" he asked.

Mamma dropped her embroidery work in her lap. "It was a disaster," she said. "A complete disaster."

Tom and I had told Mamma all about it when we had come home from school. Tom repeated the story for Papa.

"That girl is going to get an education some way," Mamma said with a determined look on her face.

Tom looked at Mamma with surprise. "You can't make anybody do something they don't want to do," he said. "Mr. Standish tried real hard, but it didn't do any good."

Mamma stared hard at Tom as if she'd never seen him before, and then to my astonishment, she smiled. "Maybe I can't but you can," she said. "I am sure your great brain can make that girl want to get an education, and want to look and act like a girl."

Tom thought about it and slowly nodded his head. "Maybe I could use my great brain to solve the problem," he said. Then that conniving look came into his eyes. "How much would it be worth to you and Papa? Maybe we can make a deal."

Mamma laid her embroidery on a table and stood up. She placed her hands on her hips and addressed Tom by his full name, which meant she was plenty angry.

"We will make a deal all right, Tom Dennis," she said sternly. "Your father and I aren't exactly stupid. We know you deceived us into getting you a bicycle for Christmas by pretending you'd reformed. The bicycle goes up into the attic immediately and stays there until Dotty Blake wants to get an education and starts wearing dresses. Now put your great brain to work on that."

Tom's mouth fell open as if Mamma had just told him to pack his things and leave home and never come back. "But that isn't fair," he protested.

"It is just as fair as you pretending you'd reformed," Mamma said. "And I'm sure your father will back me up."

"I second the motion," Papa said, nodding his head.

I sure felt sorry for my brother. For the first time in his life he looked as if he wished he hadn't been born with a great brain.

"The first thing you must do," Mamma said, "is to make Dotty want to learn how to read and write. This will also involve getting her father's consent. You can begin by teaching her the *ABC's* as you taught John D. before he started school."

The look of despair disappeared from Tom's face. "You mean if I teach her the *ABC's*, I get my bike back?"

"Not quite," Mamma said. "You will also teach her how to spell simple words and identify them until she can read simple sentences from Guffey's Reader."

"And I think," Papa said, "that Dotty should be able to count and write the numerals from one to twenty-five before you get your bicycle back. You will, of course, have the help of Mr. Standish."

Tom held out his arms in a pleading gesture. "You are both asking for a miracle," he protested.

"Then let your great brain perform one," Mamma said.

"We are going to follow Dotty," Tom said to me the next day on the way home from school.

It seemed like a silly thing to do, but I was so curious I

didn't ask any questions. We followed Dotty down Main Street. Then we saw her turn suddenly and run behind the Community Church.

"What is she doing?" I asked.

"Shut up and follow me," Tom said.

We sneaked down the side of the Community Church. Tom peeked around the corner.

"Just as I expected," he whispered.

I wanted to know what he expected, so I peeked around the corner. I saw Dotty sitting on the ground with her back against the rear of the building. She had her knees doubled up and her head cradled in her arms. Her shoulders were shaking, and she was crying.

"She isn't a wild creature like Papa said," Tom whispered. "Wild creatures don't cry. That makes it easier."

"Easier for what?" I asked, completely puzzled.

"To get my bike out of the attic," Tom said. "Now back to Main Street."

Dotty came out of the alley and began to whistle as she walked across the street and down the other side.

"I don't get it," I said. "First she cries and now she's acting happy as a bird."

"That is because she doesn't want her father to know," Tom said.

Tom put his great brain to work but didn't tell me anything until Saturday afternoon. I went with him to our barn, where he saddled up Dusty.

"Are we going for a ride?" I asked.

"You can't come," Tom said. "I am going to put the first part of my great brain's plan into operation."

Tom saw Dotty pulling weeds in the front yard of the

adobe house. He rode Dusty at a gallop until he got in front of the house. He got off the mustang where Dotty couldn't see him and unloosened the cinch on the saddle.

"Mind helping me?" he called to her. "Dusty always blows up his belly when I saddle him so the cinch won't be too tight. I'm afraid to ride him at a gallop."

It was a lie, but Dotty didn't know. She came through the front gate. She talked softly to Dusty and rubbed his nose. "I'll get his mind off it," she said.

Tom pulled the cinch tight and fastened the buckle. "Thanks," he said. "The cinch is good and tight now."

"He's a beautiful mustang," Dotty said as she patted Dusty on the neck.

"Like to ride him?" Tom asked.

Dotty smiled for the first time since Tom had known her. "I'd love to," she said.

Her blue eyes were bright as she dismounted from Dusty. "He sure is a well-gaited horse," she said.

"You know a lot about horses, don't you," Tom said.

"I should," she said. "I was raised with them. I just love horses. They are the only friends I ever had except a dog we had once."

"You don't like it here in Adenville, do you?" Tom asked.

"I hate it," Dotty said with her blue eyes cold as steel. "Pa and me ain't free anymore. He has to work all day in that shop, where I know he's dyin' inside. I gotta go to school. Me and Pa don't belong here."

"But you are here," Tom said, "and should try to make the best of it. I'll be your friend if you let me. And if you do, I'll let you ride Dusty every Saturday afternoon. Not just a short ride like today but a good long ride."

That night after supper Tom made his announcement. "I made friends with Dotty Blake today," he said.

Papa stopped reading a book. Aunt Bertha stopped darning socks. Mamma stopped knitting.

"Thank the Lord," Mamma said. "At least the poor thing has one friend."

"She is not a poor thing," Tom said with rebuke in his voice. "She is just a kid who never had a chance to be friends with anybody but horses. That is how I made friends with her. I let her ride Dusty this afternoon."

"How is it going in school for her?" Papa asked.

"She won't learn anything," Tom said. "She just sits there and refuses to try no matter how patient Mr. Standish is. But don't worry, Papa, my great brain is working on it."

"In that case," Papa said, smiling at Mamma, "we have nothing to worry about."

Tom took immediate advantage of this. "Of course, my great brain would work faster and better if there was some kind of reward in it for me," he said.

"You will get two rewards," Mamma said. "First, you will get your bicycle back, and second, you will get the best reward a person can get, in helping another person who needs help."

From the look on Tom's face I could tell he didn't think that was much of a reward.

Tom and I were the only kids in school who talked to Dotty during morning and afternoon recess. I was as embarrassed as all get out, because if there was one thing a fellow didn't do in Adenville, it was to have anything to do with girls. But it didn't seem to bother Tom. Monday after school

41

he walked part way home with Dotty, while I tagged along behind. We stopped in front of our house.

"Come over tonight after supper," Tom said, "and I'll show you a picture of the most beautiful horse you've ever seen. His name is Black Beauty."

"I'll ask Pa," Dotty promised, and then she left us.

"What are you going to do?" I asked Tom.

"Put the second part of my great brain's plan into action," Tom said.

That night after Mamma and Aunt Bertha had finished the supper dishes, we were all sitting in the parlor.

"I invited Dotty to come here tonight," Tom said. "I don't know if she'll come or not. But if she does, I don't want anybody staring at her. I want everybody to pretend that a girl wearing boy's clothing is a common thing."

Mamma looked up from her knitting. "I'm glad you invited her," she said. "And we certainly wouldn't do anything to embarrass the girl."

"What have you got in mind?" Papa asked.

"I'm going to make Dotty wish she could read," Tom answered.

Just then the front door bell rang. Tom went to open the door. Dotty came into the parlor. Tom introduced her to Mamma and Aunt Bertha. She had already met Papa.

Tom walked with Dotty to our book case. "I promised to show you a picture of the most beautiful horse you've ever seen," he said as he opened the book case.

He took out my copy of *Black Beauty* and sat down on the floor with Dotty. He showed her the cover picture of the beautiful black horse with his bright black coat, one white foot, and white star on his forehead.

42

"Gosh!" Dotty exclaimed. "He is a beauty."

"There are more pictures in the book," Tom said, "from the time he was just a colt being nursed by his mother."

Tom opened the book and showed Dotty the colored pictures.

"I didn't know they had books about horses," Dotty said.

Tom waved his hand toward the book case. "There are books about everything in this world," he said.

"What does it say in the book about Black Beauty?" Dotty asked eagerly.

"This is the story of Black Beauty from the time he was just a young colt. Anna Sewell, who wrote the book, grew up with horses and loved them very much. Just like you. But she lets Black Beauty tell his own story."

"How can a horse do that?" Dotty asked, frowning.

"I told you anything can happen in a book. Can you imagine if a horse could talk?"

Dotty thought for a moment. "Maybe," she said.

"That is what the author does in this book," Tom explained. "She not only lets Black Beauty talk to his mother and other horses so you can understand what he says, but also made him so he can understand what people say. Of course, he couldn't talk to people, but he could understand what they said. And he tells the story of his life just as you or I would tell the story of our lives."

Tom opened the book to the first chapter. "The title of the first chapter is 'My Early Home,' " he said. "Now you've got to imagine Black Beauty is telling you his life story. Ready?"

"Ready," Dotty said as she shut her eyes.

Dotty sat in a trance as Tom read aloud to her. I found myself listening with great interest although I'd read the

43

book many times. Papa let his pipe go out, Mamma stopped her knitting, Aunt Bertha sat with her hands in her lap, until Tom came to the end of chapter four.

"And that is how Black Beauty came to Birtwick Park and met Merrylegs and Ginger," he said. "I think I'd better take you home now."

Dotty was very reluctant to leave. "What happened to Black Beauty next?" she asked.

"If you could read," Tom said, "I could lend you the book and you could read it. But you can't read and it is getting late. Come tomorrow night and I'll read some more to you."

"T.D. and his great brain continue to amaze me," Papa said after Tom and Dotty had left.

Tom continued to read *Black Beauty* to Dotty every night until Friday. When school let out, we walked part of the way home with her again, stopping in front of our house.

"Gosh, Tom," Dotty said, "I can't wait until tonight to find out what happened to Black Beauty next." Then she clapped her hands with joy. "And tomorrow I get to ride Dusty again."

Tom shook his head, and his face was very serious. "I'm afraid you'll never find out what happened to Black Beauty or ever get to ride Dusty again," he said.

I couldn't have been more surprised if he had suddenly kicked Dotty on the behind.

Her lips began to tremble, and she almost burst out crying. "Why?" she whispered. "What did I do?"

"It isn't what you did," Tom said. "It is what you didn't do. You aren't even trying to learn anything in school. You won't even try to learn how to read and write."

44

"What has that got to do with it?" Dotty asked.

"Everything," Tom answered. "I got a brand-new bike for Christmas. And do you know where it is? I'll tell you. It is up in our attic. And do you know why it is up in our attic? I'll tell you. Because of you."

"Me?" Dotty asked. She looked at Tom as if my brother had suddenly gone plumb loco.

"My mother and father want you to learn how to read and write and won't give me back my bike until you do," Tom said.

"What business is it of theirs?" Dotty asked as she straightened up with that too-proud-to-be-helped look on her face.

"They made it their business because your father doesn't care if you grow up ignorant like him," Tom said, passing out insults as if he made a habit of it. "Wouldn't you like to learn how to read, so you could read wonderful stories like *Black Beauty?*"

"Sure," Dotty said, "but my Pa don't want me to learn to read and write." Then she looked as if she didn't have a friend in this world. "And I can't go against my Pa," she sobbed. Then she turned and ran down the street, and I knew she was crying.

"Boy!" I said to my brother. "If Papa and Mamma knew what you just said to poor Dotty, they would give you the silent treatment for a whole year."

"It is all a part of my great brain's plan," Tom said. "Now we can go see her father."

Tom walked boldly into Mr. Stout's shop with me following. Dotty's father was mending a bridle. Tom looked at the back of Mr. Blake's head. "I'm Tom Fitzgerald," he said. "I want to talk to you, Mr. Blake."

45

Dotty's father turned around on the stool and rubbed a finger across his yellow mustache. "Dotty has told me about you," he said.

"Know where she is now?" Tom asked.

Mr. Blake shrugged his shoulders. "Home, I guess," he said.

"You guessed right but only half of it," Tom said. "She is home crying her eyes out, and it is all your fault. Oh, she won't be crying when you get home. She'll pretend that everything is just fine."

"Whadya mean my fault?" Mr. Blake asked amazed.

"I told her I wouldn't read to her anymore and she couldn't ride Dusty anymore," Tom said.

"But you can't do that," Mr. Blake said. "All she talks about is that book you're readin' to her and gettin' to ride that horse."

"If I can't ride my bike on account of you," Tom said, "I'm not going to let Dotty ride Dusty." Then he told Mr. Blake about the deal he'd made with Papa and Mamma.

"Nuthin' I hates worse'n meddlers," Mr. Blake said. "What business is it of your ma and pa how I raise my daughter?"

"Dotty wants to learn," Tom said. "She wants to get an education. But she isn't going to try because she believes you don't want her to learn anything."

Mr. Blake slumped back on his stool. "I reckon as how that is what I made her think," he said. "I kept tellin' her I didn't hold with book learnin', but only because I didn't want the other kids makin' fun of her."

"Dotty has a good mind," Tom said. "She could learn quickly if she tried. I'll bet Mr. Standish would let her skip a grade almost every year if she tried. But she isn't going to try as long as she thinks you don't want her to get an education."

Mr. Blake looked steadily at Tom. "What do you want me to do?" he asked.

"I'll make a deal with you," Tom said. "You tell Dotty you've changed your mind and want her to get an education. Tell her she must come to my house every weekday night for an hour and for two hours on Saturday mornings. That is your part of the deal. If you agree, I'll read to Dotty for half an hour every weekday night from *Black Beauty* and other books and help her with her lessons the other half hour. And I'll tutor her for two hours every Saturday. And I'll let her ride Dusty every Saturday afternoon for as long as she wants."

Mr. Blake stood up and grabbed his crutch. He hobbled to the counter and held out his hand. "You've got yourself a deal, boy," he said.

Dotty was smiling when she entered our parlor that evening just a few minutes after seven.

"We will study for half an hour," Tom said, "and then I'll read to you from *Black Beauty* for half an hour."

"Pa told me," she said and looked as if she'd just been given every present under a Christmas tree. "I'm ready to start learning."

Tom had got my old set of blocks with the alphabet on them from our attic and had put them on the floor. He told Dotty to sit down opposite him on the floor with the blocks between them. He explained to her each of the blocks had a different letter of the alphabet on it.

"We will start with the first letter of the alphabet," he said as he picked up the block with an *A* on it. "This is a vowel and called an *A* like in the word hay. It has other sounds when used in other words. We'll study them later.

47

Look at the letter close, and say out loud five times, 'This is an *A*.'"

Then Tom pushed a ruled notebook over to Dotty and handed her a pencil.

"Now print the letter *A* in the notebook just like it is on the block ten times," he said.

Tom continued teaching Dotty the alphabet this way until the half hour was up. By that time she had memorized *A* through *G*. She could pronounce them, write them in the notebook, and when Tom mixed up all the blocks on the floor, pick them out in alphabetical order. Tom was right. Dotty had a good mind.

Then Tom read *Black Beauty* to Dotty for half an hour, during which she sat spellbound with her eyes closed.

The next morning Dotty came to our house at ten o'clock, right after Tom and I had finished our Saturday chores. Tom was teaching Dotty more letters when the front door bell rang. I opened the door. There stood Sammy Leeds. He saw Dotty and Tom before I could step onto our front porch and shut the door. I could see Basil, Parley Benson, and Danny Forester standing on the front lawn.

"We're going down to the blacksmith shop to watch Mr. Huddle," Sammy said. "You and Tom want to come along?"

"We can't go now," I said. "Tom is helping Dotty."

I knew from the triumphant look on Sammy's face that I'd said the wrong thing.

Tom continued teaching Dotty the alphabet until the hour was up, and then he read *Black Beauty* to her for more than an hour until he'd finished it, just before our lunchtime.

"Starting Monday I'll begin reading you the story of Cinderella," he promised. "You can come and get Dusty right after lunch and have him all afternoon."

48

After lunch Tom and I went to the Smiths' vacant lot, where the kids were playing one-o-cat. The game stopped immediately as they crowded around us.

"Surprised to see you here, Tom," Sammy said slyly. "We didn't think we'd see much of you anymore, now that you've started playing with girls."

Jimmie Peterson hitched up his britches, which were one size too big for him. "Only sissies play with girls," he said.

If Jimmie hadn't been younger and smaller than Tom, he would have got a punch on the nose for saying it. But I could tell from the looks on the other kids' faces, they were all thinking the same thing.

"I don't play with girls," Tom said.

"I don't know what else you would call it," Sammy said. "Britches Dotty comes to your house every night and even on Saturdays. And you let her ride Dusty."

Parley Benson pushed his coon-skin cap up on his head. "Next thing we know Tom will be playing jacks and hop-scotch with Britches Dotty and might even start playing with dolls instead of with us boys."

I figured for sure that Tom would challenge Parley to a fight, but he didn't.

"You are one kid in town I haven't whipped yet," he said, "but I'll get around to it one of these days. You fellows have got a right to be suspicious. But when I tell you what happened you'll know that T.D. Fitzgerald isn't a sissy. You haven't seen me riding my new bike for a week, have you?"

The kids all shook their heads. Then Tom explained to them about Papa and Mamma taking away his bike and what he had to do to get it back.

Danny Forester was so shocked his eyelid that usually remained half shut suddenly flipped open. "You might as well kiss your bike good-bye," he said.

"You said it," Sammy said. "Teaching that dumb–dumb to read and write is impossible."

Even Parley now seemed sympathetic. "And getting Britches Dotty to wear dresses is even more impossible," he said.

"I know it sounds impossible," Tom said, "but with my great brain, I can do it. I'll have my bike back in no time."

Monday morning Mr. Standish started giving the first graders their lesson. "I don't suppose, Dotty," he said as if he knew it was hopeless, "that you've changed your mind about getting an education."

Dotty stood up. She looked proud. "I can go to the blackboard and write the letters of the alphabet up to the letter *O*," she said.

Mr. Standish just stood with his mouth open as Dotty did it.

Tom had told me that he thought by reading the story of Cinderella to Dotty, it would make her want to dress and act like a girl, but it didn't. He looked so dejected a week later during supper that Mamma couldn't help but notice.

"What is bothering you, Tom D.?" she asked.

"I've got Dotty getting an education so fast that Mr. Standish might be able to promote her into the third grade next year," Tom said. "But even my great brain can't figure out a way to make her want to wear dresses and act like a girl."

I was dumbfounded. It was the first time I'd ever heard my brother admit his great brain didn't know everything.

50

"Maybe you need a woman's help," Mamma said.

"I could sure use it," Tom said.

I was surprised the next evening after supper when Mamma started using her sewing machine. She had never used it before at night. She came into the parlor, where Tom was teaching Dotty how to spell and pronounce words phonetically.

"I wonder if I could borrow Dotty for a few moments," Mamma said. "I'm making a dress and some things for a girl her size and need to do some measuring."

Dotty went into the dining room with Mamma. It seemed to me that Mamma was doing a lot of measuring and writing down the size of Dotty's waist and everything else. She even asked Dotty the size of the cowboy boots she was wearing.

Mamma spent all day Thursday and Friday at her sewing machine, leaving all the housework and cooking to Aunt Bertha. She was still at it on Saturday morning when Dotty came for her lessons with Tom.

"I'm sorry, Dotty," Mamma said as she came into the parlor, "but I want you to do me a favor and try on a dress and some things for me."

I could tell by this time that Dotty would have jumped off the Adenville Bank building if Mamma had asked her. She followed Mamma into her bedroom. Mamma told us when Papa came home for lunch what had happened in the bedroom. First she told Dotty to strip.

"I ain't never taken my clothes off in front of anybody but my ma," Dotty protested.

"Haven't is the proper word and not ain't," Mamma said. "Just pretend I am your mother."

Dotty took off her Levi britches, boy's shirt, cowboy

51

boots, and all the rest of her clothes. Then Mamma helped her get dressed with the things she'd made, and a pair of shoes, and a few other things Mamma had bought at the Z.C.M.I. store. A pretty gingham dress was the last thing Mamma helped Dotty put on. Then Mamma stood Dotty in front of the full-length mirror on her vanity.

"Look at yourself, Dotty," she said. "That is the real you."

Dotty stared at her reflection in the mirror with a stunned expression. "I look almost pretty," she said in a whisper.

"You are a girl, my dear, and girls are meant to look pretty," Mamma said.

Dotty patted the dress gently with her hands. "I never knew dresses could be so pretty," she said.

"Everything you have on and several other dresses and pretty things I have made are all for you," Mamma said. "You are the girl I was talking about."

Then Dotty began to cry. She threw her arms around Mamma. "I wish I could take them, but I can't."

"It isn't charity," Mamma said, patting Dotty on the head. "There is much more happiness in giving than in receiving. You will make me very happy by taking them. And happier still if you'll let me be a sort of foster mother to you. Somebody you can come and talk to about things you don't want to talk about to your father. Someone who will love you as your dear mother must have loved you."

"I can't on account of my pa," Dotty sobbed. "He never really loved me because I was a girl, and he wanted a son. That's why I always tried to be as much like a boy as I could. Pa let me get an education after Tom told him off good. But——"

"My son told your father off?" Mamma asked.

52

"He sure did," Dotty said. "Pa was so upset about it when he came home from work that day, he couldn't eat his supper."

"Well," Mamma said, "Tom D. isn't the only one who told off your father. I had quite a chat with him the other day. And you are wrong about him not loving you. He loves you very much."

When Mamma returned to the parlor with Dotty, my eyeballs must have popped six inches out of their sockets and then back again. Tom was plenty surprised too.

"You're pretty," he said sort of stunned like. "Just like Cinderella. You sure aren't Britches Dotty anymore."

Dotty smiled shyly. "Thanks, Tom."

"Now to the corral," Mamma said, "and I'll prove to you, Dotty, how much your father really loves you."

I couldn't figure out why Mamma had got Dotty all dressed up like a girl to take her to our corral until we reached the gate. There in the corral was a strange sorrel mare, who had a white star on her forehead. She had on a saddle and bridle. She didn't prick up her ears like a mare would upon seeing people. She just stood there sort of listless.

"Her name is Star," Mamma said to Dotty. "I met Mr. and Mrs. Smedley in town a few days ago. They own a big ranch about five miles from town. The mare belonged to their daughter, Joan, who died of pneumonia just before Christmas. Mr. Smedley told me how much Star missed her mistress. He said the mare would hardly eat and was pining away from a broken heart. I told him I knew a girl who loved horses very, very much. A girl who needed the mare as much as the mare needed somebody to love."

Dotty looked at Mamma with her big blue eyes full of

53

wonder and hope. "You mean that mare is for me?" she asked breathlessly.

"Maybe," Mamma said. "A ranch hand from the Bar S brought the mare into town yesterday. I had him put Star in the livery stable and not deliver her until a few moments ago."

"You said maybe," Dotty said. The hope left her eyes.

"There are three conditions," Mamma said. "First, I promised Mr. and Mrs. Smedley the mare would have a good home. Right at this moment Mr. Jamison, the carpenter, is putting shingles on that old barn in back of the adobe house and doing any other repairs that might be needed. You and the boys can clean out the barn and make it into a nice stable for Star. Mr. Harmon at the Z.C.M.I. store is sending over a nosebag, a brush, and a curry comb. Mr. Brown of the Hay, Grain, and Feed Store is sending over a bag of oats. Several people who own livestock are sending over bales of hay. That takes care of the first condition. Star will have a good home."

"But Pa won't take charity," Dotty protested.

"During my talk with your father, I convinced him there is a big difference between outright charity and just being neighborly," Mamma said. "Now for the second condition. Star will need loving care until she becomes as fond of you as she was of Joan."

"I promise to love her and take good care of her," Dotty said quickly, as the look of hope returned to her blue eyes.

"And now for the last condition," Mamma said. "You must accept the wardrobe I've prepared for you and dress and act like a girl and make friends with girls your age in town."

"Pa don't want me to dress and act like a girl," she sobbed.

"Your father has changed his mind about that," Mamma said. "And you see that saddle on Star? It is a present from

54

your father. He is going to pay Mr. Stout a little each month for it."

Dotty threw her arms around Mamma's neck and kissed her.

Boy, it was sure getting mushy around there, but the worst was still to come.

"I know you are dying to ride Star," Mamma said. "I think we can make allowances for your old clothes when you are riding Star. So off you go and change."

Then that worst part of the mushy business came. Dotty looked at Tom and walked over to him. And I'll be a four-legged frog if she didn't kiss him right on the lips.

Poor old T.D.'s ears lit up like red-hot coals in a fireplace. The shock petrified his great brain. He just stood there with a dummy's expression on his face as Mamma and Dotty walked toward our house. I waited for Tom to come out of his shock, and when he didn't, I grabbed him by the shoulders and began shaking him.

"Did it hurt that much?" I asked.

I knew I would have probably dropped dead if a girl had kissed me.

Tom came out of it sudden-like. "Don't be silly," he said. "Dotty was just showing her appreciation for all my great brain did for her."

"Boy!" I said. "I hope I never do anything that makes a girl appreciate it that much. If the fellows knew you'd been kissed by a girl, they would never speak to you again."

"I'm sure not going to tell them, and neither are you," Tom said.

My little brain saw a golden opportunity to get even with Tom for all the times he'd swindled me.

55

"Oh, I don't know about that," I said casually. "I think the fellows ought to know you've been kissed by a girl."

Tom knew I had him over a barrel. "All right, J.D.," he said. "How much not to tell?"

"How about doing all my chores for a week?" I asked.

"It's a deal." Tom answered so quickly I knew I hadn't asked for enough.

"And how about letting me use your bike for a whole week?" I asked.

"All right," Tom said.

Boy, I was enjoying this so much I couldn't stop. "And we just might add ten cents in cash before we seal the bargain," I said.

"Ten cents it is," Tom said. "But before we shake hands on the deal, I just want you to know that it is going to break Papa's and Mamma's hearts when I tell them they have a son who is a blackmailer. And because I don't want to associate with blackmailers, I'm giving you the silent treatment from now on."

I sure didn't want Papa and Mamma to think they had raised a blackmailer, and I knew from past experience that I'd rather be dead than have Tom give me the silent treatment.

"Forget the whole deal," I said. "My word of honor I won't tell."

"Then you admit it was a shameful thing to try and blackmail your own brother?" Tom asked.

"Yes," I said.

"So shameful you should be punished for it?" Tom asked.

"I guess so," I said.

"Because you're my brother, and I love you, I'm going to let you off easy," Tom said. "Give me your word of honor

that you'll never tell the fellows Dotty kissed me, and do all my chores for a week, and we'll call it even."

"Word of honor," I said, crossing my heart.

That evening after supper while Mamma and Aunt Bertha were doing the dishes, Tom and I were sitting on the floor in the parlor. Papa was smoking his pipe.

"You have done a wonderful thing for Dotty Blake," Papa said to Tom.

"Thanks, Papa," Tom said. Then he winked at me as he kept his face turned away from Papa. "You know, J.D., it is just too bad I won't be tutoring Dotty anymore. Without my help Mr. Standish might not let her skip the second grade next year."

"What's this?" Papa asked as he removed his pipe from his mouth. "Of course, you will continue to help the girl."

Tom turned around and faced Papa. "Why should I?" he asked. "I kept my part of the bargain with you and Mamma, and I have my bike back."

"You will continue to help Dotty, and that is final," Papa said.

Tom shrugged. "All right, Papa, but you'll have to fix it up with Mamma when the trouble starts. You and Mamma can expect me to get into a fight with some kid almost every day. And I don't want to be punished for something that is your fault."

"And just why should you be getting into a fight every day?" Papa asked.

Tom stood up and folded his arms on his chest. "When you were my age, you didn't have anything to do with girls, did you?"

"Well, no," Papa answered.

"And when you were my age, any other boy who had anything to do with girls was called a sissy, wasn't he?" Tom asked.

"You could say that," Papa agreed.

"And if any boy had called you a sissy, you would have fought him. Right, Papa?"

Papa squirmed in his chair. "I suppose I would have," he said.

"Well, what do you think is going to happen to me if I go on seeing Dotty and helping her?" Tom asked. "Every kid in town is going to start making fun of me and calling me a sissy. That means I'll be getting into a fight almost every day. And I might even have to beat up a few kids smaller than me, just to make them stop calling me a sissy."

"But you were helping Dotty before and didn't get into any fights over it," Papa said.

"Only because I explained to the other kids it was the only way I could get back my bike," Tom said. "Now I've got my bike back. There is no excuse for me helping Dotty."

Papa rubbed the stem of his pipe on his teeth. "There must be some way," he said. "Your mother and I want to help that girl all we can."

"There is a way, all right," Tom said. "If the kids thought I was getting paid for tutoring Dotty, they would understand—because they all know I only use my great brain to make money or to get something. But if I tell them I'm getting paid when I'm not getting paid, that would be lying. And lying is worse than fighting."

Papa was a smart man. He took out his purse and looked at Tom. "How much, T.D.?" he asked. "How about half a dollar to go on tutoring Dotty from now until school lets out?"

59

"Better make it a dollar," Tom said. "Some of the kids might think it's worth more than half a dollar. But if I can show them a whole silver dollar, I'm sure they will understand."

"All right, T.D." Papa handed Tom a whole silver dollar. "But on one condition. I would prefer your mother didn't know about this. She has never been a boy and might not understand."

CHAPTER THREE

The Time Papa Got Lost

WHEN SCHOOL STARTS, a fellow always feels as if the summer vacation will never come. He starts by counting the months until the Christmas holidays. Then he starts counting the weeks until May. Then he starts counting the days, and each day seems as long as those months before the Christmas holidays. But there is one good thing about the sun that parents and teachers can't do a darn thing about. It comes up every morning, and it sets every night. Nobody can stop that wonderful last day of school from coming around at last.

Tom graduated from the sixth grade. I graduated from the fourth grade. I guess Mr. Standish thought he was the

61

greatest teacher in the world when he announced that he would start Dotty in the third grade next fall. Mr. Standish had to teach all six grades, and I doubt if Dotty would ever have made it if it hadn't been for Tom tutoring her. She learned more from Tom during a half hour in the evening than she learned in school all day. But Tom seemed satisfied to let the teacher take all the credit. He had his dollar.

Dotty had turned into a real girl, except when it came to riding Star. And she made friends with girls her age even though they weren't in the same grade. I guess she made friends so easily because she was a sort of celebrity. She was the only girl in town who had whipped a boy bigger than her in a fair and square fight. The dresses Mamma made for Dotty made her one of the best-dressed girls in town. And she learned how to play jacks, hopscotch, jump the rope, and even to play with dolls.

Two days after our school let out, Sweyn came home from the Catholic Academy. I was never so disappointed in my life. He sure had changed since Christmas. He was wearing long trousers with the suit Mamma had sent him for Easter. And he started off by calling Papa, Dad, and Mamma, Mom. That was all right with me because it didn't seem to bother our parents. But when he started calling Tom and me "Old Man" instead of by our initials, that was going too far.

Tom and I were trying to be nice to him on his first evening at home. "You can ride my bike whenever you want," Tom said generously.

"Thanks, Old Man, but that's kid stuff," Sweyn said.

"Want to see my jumping frog?" I asked.

"Thanks, Old Man, but that's kid stuff," Sweyn said.

That got me. "I'm not an old man," I said. "I'm just a kid."

"It is an expression us city folks use," Sweyn said with a laugh.

Papa, Mamma, and Aunt Bertha began to laugh too. I knew right then I'd have to put up with Sweyn calling me old man all summer.

This was bad enough, but the day after he got home, Sweyn pulled the dirtiest trick he could on Tom and me. He started going with a girl, and of all the girls he had to pick, it was that stuck-up Marie Vinson. If ever a fellow felt like disowning a brother, it was me. All I heard from my friends was, "Sweyn's got a girl. Sweyn's got a girl." If Sweyn wanted to disgrace me and Tom, why couldn't he have kicked a dog, or beat up an old lady, or something not as bad as going with a girl.

A few days after Sweyn had arrived, Papa told us we would leave on Monday for our annual camping trip. At least for a week I'd get out of town, where I was now known along with Tom as the kids who had a brother who was going with a girl. Papa announced the trip on Saturday during supper.

"I've closed the *Advocate* for a week," he said. "We will leave early Monday morning."

"Where are we going this year?" Tom asked eagerly.

"Why not up Beaver Canyon, where we went last year?" Papa asked. "The fishing was excellent, and the hunting very good."

We left Adenville early Monday morning. Tom and I rode on the seat of the buckboard with Papa, who was driving our team of Bess and Dick. We had all our supplies and tent securely fastened to the bed of the buckboard in back of the seat. Sweyn rode Dusty. We traveled a logging road along the foothills of the Wasatch range of mountains until we came to

63

the mouth of Beaver Canyon. The canyon got its name from the beaver dams at the head of the river that flowed down the canyon. We watered the horses and then ate the lunch Mamma had prepared for us.

I stuffed myself on the fried chicken, hard-boiled eggs, bread and butter sandwiches, cake, and pie that Mamma had put in a cardboard shoe box. I knew from experience this would be our last bite of good cooking until we returned home. When we had eaten all we could, Papa stood up and patted his stomach.

"No sense in going on a fishing and camping trip if you don't rough it," he said. "Throw away what you can't eat, boys."

The only food Papa allowed us to keep was flour, salt and pepper, a sack of potatoes, bacon, a case of pork and beans, a small sack of onions, sugar, coffee, cans of condensed milk, and a small sack of dried beans. We expected to arrive at our destination in time to catch a mess of fish for supper.

I was admiring the canyon as we drove up it. Pine and cedar trees were intermingled with aspens and cottonwoods. Some of the trees were growing out of cracks in cliffs and ledges. There were wild flowers. All of them had a great smell you never got in town. Blue jays cawed at us, and we could hear mountain canaries singing.

Papa seemed much more concerned about the road. "This road looks well traveled compared with what it was last year," he said.

"Maybe they have put on more men at the logging camp on top of the plateau," Tom said.

"I doubt it," Papa said. "You can see this road has been traveled by buggies, wagons, and buckboards."

We discovered why the road was so well traveled when

we arrived at the place where we had camped last year. There were buggies, wagons, buckboards, tents, and people all over the place.

"What in the name of Jupiter are all these people doing here?" Papa demanded, as if they were all poaching on his private property. "With all the places there are to fish in Utah, why did everybody who owns a fishing pole suddenly decide to choose this particular place?"

It wasn't hard for a fellow with a little brain like me to figure out. The year before we'd brought home about four dozen beautiful rainbow and German brown trout packed in wet mud and grass. Papa had insisted we lay them out on our front lawn to wash off the mud and grass with the hose. A big crowd gathered on the sidewalk in front of our house. I remembered how Papa had told them about his perfect place to fish in Beaver Canyon.

Tom had been thinking the same thing. "Maybe you shouldn't have told so many people about this place last year," he said.

"Well, you would think people would have the decency to respect a man's private fishing and camping ground," Papa said.

Papa could certainly exaggerate. It was public land, and all those people had as much right to be there as we did. We found a place to camp and pitched our tent. Then we went fishing, but the water was muddy from a rainstorm farther up the canyon. We didn't even get a bite. We ate a supper of cold pork and beans out of cans and sourdough biscuits we baked in our Dutch oven.

"The stream is all fished out," Papa said as we finished eating. "That settles it. We will leave in the morning and find a place to fish and hunt where no white man has ever been."

65

The next morning we followed the logging road up the canyon for about four miles, where the road branched off to the left up Beaver Canyon, and there was another canyon to the right. I thought Papa had suddenly gone crazy when he turned the team to the right and started up a dry creek bed.

Sweyn rode Dusty over to the side of the buckboard. "Where are you going?" he asked. "There isn't even a road or a trail."

"Exactly," Papa said smugly. "Where there is no road or trail, there are no people."

Even Tom with his great brain was impressed by Papa's daring when he leaned back and looked up at the towering sides of the canyon.

"Are you going to try and cross the mountain?" he asked.

Papa at that moment must have fancied himself another Jedediah Smith, the Yankee Methodist minister who had explored most of the Utah Territory with a Bible in one hand and a rifle in the other.

"We will find ourselves a virgin stream and valley on the other side," Papa said confidently.

Tom jumped down from the buckboard. "I think I'll walk," he said. "Make it easier on the team."

Papa started up the dry creek bed with Sweyn in the lead acting as a scout. I turned around to make sure Tom was following us. I was surprised to see him carving something on a tree where we'd turned off the road. I was even more surprised as I watched him gather up some rocks and lay them on the bank of the dry creek bed.

We continued up the canyon with Tom lagging behind. The only time Tom caught up to us was when Papa stopped so we could roll boulders and logs out of the way of the buckboard. The big logs and boulders that were too heavy Sweyn roped with his lariat and with Dusty's help pulled them out of the way.

My curiosity got the better of me as I turned around several times and saw Tom using his jackknife on a tree or making piles of rocks. I jumped out of the buckboard and joined him.

"What are you doing?" I asked.

"Just carving my initials on a few trees," Tom said.

"Why?" I asked. "Nobody will ever see them."

"I wouldn't say that," Tom said. "Someday they might build a road up this canyon, and I can prove we were the first ones who ever went up it. Maybe it will make us famous as pioneers."

"That is a peach of an idea," I had to admit. "But what are you doing with those rocks?"

"Looking for gold," he said.

"But that is silly," I said. "All these canyons have been covered by prospectors."

Tom looked a little ashamed of himself. "Maybe it is silly," he said, "but it helps to pass the time. Don't say anything to Papa. He might think it's silly."

"All right," I said, "but I'm not going to walk all the way to the top of this mountain."

We continued up the canyon with Tom, Sweyn, and me rolling boulders and logs out of the way for the rest of the day. Just before dusk we stopped, and believe me we had to stop. There was a cliff rising up from the dry creek bed stretching from one side of the canyon to the other that must have been thirty feet high. During a heavy rainstorm, when the dry creek bed became a stream, and the cliff a waterfall, it must have been something to see. But right now all it meant to me was that we had to turn around and go back.

"We'll camp here tonight," Papa said, as if there wasn't an impossible barrier in our way.

We couldn't find a spring so Sweyn rationed the water in the small water barrel tied on our buckboard. We ate mulligan stew made from sliced potatoes, onions, and pieces of bacon all boiled in water in a big frying pan and some more sourdough biscuits with honey.

The next morning we had fried potatoes and bacon and more sourdough biscuits. Then Papa studied both sides of the canyon.

"We'll go up the left side," he said.

Sweyn looked at the steep slope of the canyon. "That is impossible," he said. "The buckboard will tip over."

"No it won't," Papa said. "You will tie one end of your lariat under the buckboard seat to the clamp that holds the seat in place. You will snag the other end of your lariat to the pommel of your saddle, and make certain the cinch on your saddle is good and tight. You will ride Dusty upslope from me opposite the buckboard about fifteen feet. The mustang will prevent the buckboard from tipping over."

"But all our supplies will fall out of the buckboard," Sweyn protested.

"Nonsense," Papa said. "We will cover our supplies with the tent and tie the stake ropes on the tent underneath the buckboard." Papa took a deep breath. "I am enjoying teaching you boys how to rough it. It is a trick used by early pioneers to bypass such obstacles as this cliff when they had no roads."

When everything was ready, we had to go back about half a mile so the pull wouldn't be too steep for the team. Papa hadn't gone more than twenty yards when the slope of the canyon became so steep the buckboard was riding on two wheels. The only thing preventing it from tipping over was Sweyn's sure-footed mustang. I died a thousand deaths fearing the lariat would break and Papa would be dashed to death down the side of the canyon. But we finally made it to the top of the cliff and back onto the dry creek bed.

The going was pretty easy from there to the top of the mountain, which we reached just before dark. It was very cold, and after supper we all slept in our blankets in the tent.

Going down the other side of the mountain the next day was easy. We came to a mountain valley that turned out to be a fishing and hunting paradise, just like Papa had promised. There was a sparkling stream filled with trout. Small game was plentiful.

We remained in our mountain paradise for four days. We dined on quail, pheasant, sage hens, rabbits, and wild turkeys, as well as rainbow trout. Everything was perfect until the time came to leave for home.

"We'll take a shortcut out," Papa announced after we'd eaten breakfast and were breaking camp.

Tom stopped folding our tent and looked at Papa. "How can we take a shortcut when we've never been here before?" he asked.

"I've always prided myself on my sense of direction," Papa said. "We will follow this valley. It will bring us out of the mountains just a few miles above Adenville."

We finished packing and loading the buckboard and were ready to go when Tom put his hand on the front wheel.

"I'm going to walk behind, Papa," he said.

Papa looked surprised. "Why walk?" he asked. "The bottom of the valley is quite level and nothing but sagebrush and a few trees."

"I just feel like walking," Tom said.

69

Just before we stopped to camp for the night, the stream turned to a canyon on the left, and there was another canyon to the right. Papa said we'd take the canyon to the right the next morning.

"But Dad," Sweyn protested, "what will we do for water?"

"There are plenty of springs in these mountains," Papa said. "We must take the canyon to the right because Adenville lies in that direction."

Well, all I can say is that Papa was right about one thing. There were springs in those mountains with enough water for us and the horses. But it sure wasn't the way to Adenville. The canyon to the right came to a fork of two more canyons. We took the one to the right and ended up in a blind canyon. We came back and took the other canyon, and again ended up in a fork, and again took the canyon to the right. We came back and took the other canyon. Finally we came to another canyon that had a stream of water running down it.

It was a good thing we camped on high ground that night because we had the worst cloudburst I'd ever seen or heard. The rain came down as if poured from giant buckets in the sky. The river was a raging torrent of water when we came out of the tent in the morning, although the rain had stopped.

"There is nothing like roughing it," Papa said cheerfully as he made sourdough biscuits with the last of our flour. "I could spend all summer in these mountains, but we'd better start for home. Your mother will be worried. We are a couple of days overdue now."

Boy, did that make me feel better. I was sure that we were lost in the mountains, and all the time Papa had only been pretending to be lost to give us boys an exciting adventure.

70

Sweyn must have been thinking the same thing. "You mean we aren't lost?" he asked.

"How can a person be lost in the mountains when there is running water?" Papa asked as he pointed at the rain-swelled river. "Water runs downhill. All we have to do is to follow this river downstream, and it will lead us out of these mountains."

"Then why didn't we follow the other stream?" Sweyn asked.

"That would have taken us out on the other side of the mountains from Adenville," Papa answered.

We followed the river downstream until we came to a waterfall. Papa said we would bypass the waterfall the same way we had bypassed the cliff, by going down one side of the canyon around the waterfall with Sweyn and Dusty holding the buckboard from tipping over.

Tom and I were walking behind; Papa was sitting on the seat of the buckboard. I had my head down to see where I was stepping when I heard Sweyn scream. I looked up, and it felt as if my chest had caved in. The strain on the lariat had become too much, and it had broken. I was stunned with horror. Papa leaped from the seat of the buckboard just a second before it turned over and went tumbling down the side of the canyon, pulling the team with it.

I ran crying to Papa and threw my arms around his waist. He patted my head.

"Next time we'll take pack horses," he said calmly—as if he lost a buckboard every day of the week.

The buckboard was a total wreck, with two wheels smashed so badly they couldn't possibly be fixed. Bess was standing up and shaking with fright, but Dick kept trying to stand up only to fall down and was screaming something awful. We made our way down the steep slope of the canyon to where the horses were. Papa unhitched Bess and had Sweyn tie one end of his broken lariat around her neck and take her to one side with Dusty. Then Papa knelt down and examined poor old Dick. His face was grave as he stood up.

"His right foreleg is broken," he said. "I'll have to shoot him."

Sweyn got his .22 rifle from the holster attached to his saddle and handed it to Papa. I watched Papa put the end of the barrel in Dick's ear and then turned my head away. I heard the sound of the shot. I turned around. Dick still seemed to be moving. Papa shot him again in the head. Then the horse lay still.

Our tent was ripped in half, and our supplies were scattered all over the side of the canyon. We salvaged what we could and made a pack horse out of Bess.

Papa mounted Dusty and led the pack horse, Sweyn and I followed close behind on foot, and Tom lagged behind again.

We followed the stream downhill until afternoon of the following day. Then Papa pulled Dusty to a halt.

"Don't worry, boys," he shouted over his shoulder. "When we round that bend up ahead, you'll be able to see the mouth of the canyon."

I felt cheered up enough to start whistling. My whistling stopped suddenly as we rounded the bend in the canyon. Instead of the mouth of the canyon I saw a thousand-foot high wall of granite forming another blind canyon. The river ran downhill all right, just as Papa said it would, but this river went right under that thousand-foot wall of granite, forming an underground river.

72

Papa dismounted. He folded his arms and stared at that granite wall as if it had a lot of nerve being there.

I knew we were hopelessly lost and began to cry.

"Stop that blubbering, J.D.," Tom said. "It will upset Papa."

"I think Dad is already upset," Sweyn said. "We are lost for sure. I've only about a dozen shells left for my rifle, and I doubt if Dad has any shells left for the shotgun."

"Who needs shells?" Tom asked. "Let's build a lean-to for Papa first and then set some deadfall traps."

Papa sat down on a boulder and stared at the granite cliff as though if he stared at it long enough it would disappear.

Us boys unsaddled Dusty and unpacked Bess. We put hobbles on them and turned them loose to graze.

"Dad has got us into a mess," Sweyn said as he got the axe we had salvaged from the wreck.

"If it was just a mess, I wouldn't care," I said. "But I think Papa has got us lost in these mountains."

"Crying over spilt milk won't do any good," Tom said. "We've got to make camp, and make sure we have something to eat. Let's get busy."

We followed Sweyn to a grove of aspen trees. We found two strong Y-shaped branches on them. Sweyn cut them off with the axe. Tom cut the small branches off them with his jackknife. We went back to where we were going to make our campsite. With his jackknife Tom dug two holes about six inches deep and about ten feet apart. We stuck the aspen poles in the holes with the Y on top and packed dirt around them. By that time Sweyn joined us with a straight branch of a tree from which he'd chopped off all the branches. Tom stripped enough bark from it to make thongs with his jackknife. Then we put the pole between the Y's on the poles in the ground and lashed them together with the bark. We got the piece of tent we'd salvaged and draped it over the pole between the two Y's. Then we put rocks all around the edge of the piece of tent so the wind couldn't blow it away. Next we cut some pine branches and carried them into the tent to use for a mattress.

"That will take care of Papa," Tom said. "We can sleep in our blankets around the camp fire. Now for some deadfalls."

We walked along the bank of the river until we came to a game trail used by animals that came down to the river to drink at night. While Tom carved sticks for the deadfalls, Sweyn and I found three big flat slabs of rock, which we carried to the game trail. We waited until Tom had carved the notches in the sticks to spring the trap of the deadfall. Then I picked some wild clover along the bank of the river. Tom used some blades of wild grass to tie the clover to the end of the stick that would trigger the deadfall. Then he set the figure 4 of the deadfall with three sticks together in their notches. He held the figure 4 while Sweyn and I carefully placed one end of one of the flat slabs of rock on top of it. When a rabbit or any other small game animal nibbled on the bait on the end of the bait stick, it would dislodge the notches on the other two sticks and cause the flat rock to fall on it and kill it or stun it so that it would be under the rock in the morning.

When we returned to our campsite, Papa was still sitting on the boulder. Tom and I made a camp fire. Sweyn went hunting and used two of his precious shells to kill a rabbit and one quail, which we had for supper.

I was scared and felt like crying, and Papa sure didn't help matters after we'd finished eating.

74

"I don't want to alarm you, boys," he said as he puffed on his pipe, "but things look quite serious."

Sweyn doubled up his knees and held them with his hands. "Mom certainly must have told Uncle Mark to come look for us when we didn't get back on time," he said.

"Where would he look?" Papa asked. "He had no idea where we were going except up Beaver Canyon."

"But he could find the tracks of the horses and buckboard," Sweyn said.

"You are forgetting that cloudburst we had," Papa said. "It certainly washed out any tracks made by the horses and the buckboard."

I couldn't hold back the tears any longer and began to cry. "We are going to die," I sobbed.

"We certainly aren't going to die," Papa said. "I read an article one time about a man who was lost in the Rocky Mountains for five years. He managed to live on small game, fish, pinenuts, and wild berries until finally he was rescued by some trappers." Then Papa stood up and stretched. "I think it is time to bed down now," he said.

Papa went into his lean-to. We wrapped ourselves in our blankets and lay down around the fire. Papa sure didn't make me feel any better with that story of the man lost for five years. We were going to die in these mountains. I would never see Mamma or Aunt Bertha or any of my friends again. Someday some renegade Indians might find us and scalp us and torture us to death. That would perhaps be better than living the rest of our lives in this wilderness. But we hadn't seen any sign of Indians. That meant only one thing. Someday some intrepid explorer or trapper would come across our bleached bones and wonder if they were the bones of white people or Indians. We were doomed. Doomed to die in this wilderness.

Tom touched my shoulder. "For gosh sakes, J.D.," he whispered, "stop that bawling and go to sleep."

"I can't help it," I cried softly. "We are doomed to live the rest of our lives in these mountains like Paiute Indians, eating grasshoppers, ants, wild berries, pinenuts——"

"Will you shut up with that doomed business," Tom interrupted me. "You don't think for a minute I'd let my great brain let us get lost in these mountains, do you?"

I felt like laughing and crying at the same time. What a fool I had been when I had my brother and his great brain with us.

"God bless your great brain," I said and promptly fell asleep.

The next morning we found we'd caught two rabbits in our deadfalls and four trout on our night fishing poles. We ate the trout for breakfast and saved the rabbits. Papa was very quiet. After we had finished eating, Papa went back to the boulder and sat staring at that thousand-foot-high granite cliff as if trying to come to some decision. We had just finished washing the tin plates and knives and forks when he motioned to us.

"Boys," he said as we stood in front of him. I'd never seen his face so serious. "I think we should start building a log cabin."

"How are you going to build a cabin without a saw and a hammer and nails and things?" Sweyn asked.

"The same way the early pioneers did," Papa answered. "Using the bark of aspen trees to bind the logs together and mud from the banks of the river to chink up the cracks between the logs. And there is a ledge of flat rock over there we can use to build a fireplace. We must prepare for the worst and hope for the best. It may be years before some friendly Indians or some trapper finds us."

Tom shook his head. "Isn't it silly to start building a cabin when Uncle Mark will be riding in here in a few days?" he asked.

"That is impossible," Papa said. "That cloudburst washed away all our tracks."

"No it didn't," Tom said. "I knew when we turned off the logging camp road that we might get lost. I used rocks to make markers that wouldn't wash away, and I cut markers on trees no cloudburst could destroy. That is why I was lagging behind all the time. If my calculations are correct, Uncle Mark should be riding in here in two or three days, if we just stay here. You didn't think my great brain would let us get lost, did you, Papa?"

Papa and Sweyn stared at Tom bug-eyed for a moment, and then they both began to smile happily. Papa got off the boulder and patted Tom on the shoulder.

"I'm proud of you, son," he said. "It was foolish of me to try and find a shortcut out of these mountains without marking our trail."

Then Papa had a second thought about what he had just said. He staggered back to the boulder and sat down. He covered his face with his hands as if he were going to cry.

"What's the matter with him?" Sweyn whispered.

"I don't know," Tom answered. "Suppose we find out."

Tom walked up close to Papa. "What is the matter?" he asked. "I told you we were going to be saved."

Papa raised his head up. "I'll never live this down," he cried as if being tortured. "Your mother will never forgive me for trying to take a shortcut and endangering all our lives.

77

And I can just hear people in town bringing up the subject every time some neighbor's cow wanders away. I'll be the butt of jokes for years."

Then Papa got real dramatic and held his arms out in a hopeless gesture. "That is the only answer," he cried. "I'll stay right here. Better to live out my life in this wilderness than to go back and have people point me out as the town fool. You boys return with your Uncle Mark. I'm staying right here."

Tom stared at Papa for a moment as his great brain began to click. Then he looked at Sweyn.

"Did you see me mark the trail?" he asked.

Sweyn looked surprised for a second and then smiled. "No," he answered.

Tom looked at me and winked. "Did you see me mark the trail, J.D.?"

"No," I lied.

"Well," Tom said with a shake of his head, "I sure don't remember marking our trail, and that leaves only Papa."

The look of despair on Papa's face gave way to one of hope. He looked as though he might enjoy the comforts of home more than living like a savage in the wilderness.

"Thank you, boys," he said. "Thank you from the bottom of my heart."

I figured Tom would have liked it better to be thanked from the bottom of Papa's purse but didn't say anything.

We lived for two and a half days on small game we caught in our deadfalls, fish we caught, and roasted pinenuts. On the afternoon of the third day Uncle Mark rode into our camp on his white stallion, leading two pack horses. I was never so glad to see anybody in my life. But Papa folded his arms on his chest and looked positively angry.

"What in the name of Jupiter took you so long?" he demanded. "Leaving me all this time trying to keep up the spirits of my boys?"

I didn't know what spirits Papa was talking about. He sure hadn't kept up my spirits with that story of the man lost for five years in the mountains.

Uncle Mark grinned as he dismounted. Then he looked at Papa. "If you'd just stayed in one place after you knew you were lost," he said, "instead of wandering up and down one blind canyon after another, I would have caught up with you a few days ago. It is a good thing you had sense enough to mark your trail, or I would never have found you."

"What kind of a tenderfoot do you think I am?" Papa asked as if insulted. "You certainly don't think for a moment that I'd try to take a shortcut out of these mountains without marking my trail, do you?"

Uncle Mark turned sideways so Papa couldn't see him wink at Tom. "Of course not," he said. "But you really gave me a scare when I saw the wrecked buckboard and the dead horse. It is a good thing you didn't let anybody ride in the buckboard when you tried to bypass that waterfall. They might have been killed if you had."

Papa must have forgot his wild leap from the buckboard. "I certainly wouldn't do a fool thing like that," he said.

"Gosh, T.D.," I whispered to Tom, "Papa is lying like all get out."

"Would you rather have him tell a few little white lies, or have everybody in Adenville think he was a fool?" Tom asked.

"But your great brain saved us, and Papa is taking all the credit," I protested.

"I know, and you know, and Sweyn knows, and Uncle

Mark knows I marked the trail," Tom said. "But that is as far as it will ever go. We aren't even going to tell Mamma."

I thought about it for a moment and knew Tom was right. It would be bad enough for everybody in Adenville to think Papa was a fool. But letting Mamma know she had married one would certainly break her heart.

CHAPTER FOUR

Tom Scoops Papa's Newspaper

EVERY TUESDAY IT WAS TOM'S and my job to deliver the weekly edition of Papa's newspaper. The second
Tuesday after we'd returned from our fishing and camping
trip, we entered the *Advocate* office after doing our morning
chores at home. Papa usually wrote his editorial and set the
type for it and for the advertisements during the first five days
of the week, in addition to any extra printing jobs he had. He
also set the type for news items from other Utah newspapers
which he thought might interest his readers, and national
news items received by telegraph, and the mail edition of the
New York World. He waited until Saturday to set the type for
the local news items he had collected during the week. The

81

four-page weekly newspaper was printed on Monday and delivered to subscribers on Tuesday morning.

Sweyn really thought he was something, helping Papa at
the *Advocate*, wearing long pants, a printer's apron, and a
green eye shade. The way he lorded it over Tom and me!

"It's about time you got here, Old Man," he said to Tom
as we entered the *Advocate* office with its smell of ink and
paper.

"Sorry we are late, Grandpa," Tom said, "But Mamma
made us weed the vegetable garden this morning."

Sweyn's eyes popped open. "What is this Grandpa business?" he asked.

"If I'm an old man," Tom said, "you must be my grandfather."

Boy, how I wished I could have thought of that snappy
comeback, which positively stunned my oldest brother for a
moment. Then he got a sly look on his face as he pointed at
the two neatly piled stacks of the weekly on the counter.

"Papa went to the barbershop for a haircut," he said,
"but he told me to make sure you little grade-school kids did a
good job."

From the look on Tom's face I could tell he would rather
be called Old Man than a little grade-school kid. But he
didn't say anything as he grabbed his pile of the weekly and
me the other pile. We carried them outside and Tom put his
copies in the basket on his bike. It was his job to deliver the
Advocate to the homes of all subscribers in Adenville because
he had a bicycle. It was my job to drop off all copies of the
newspaper that had yellow name stickers on them at the post
office. These were mailed. I left the rest of my copies on the
counter of the Z.C.M.I. store and on the desk at the Sheepmen's Hotel for people to buy for cash.

82

I don't know if Sweyn calling Tom and me little grade-school kids started it but after supper that night Tom got what Papa called growing pains. Mamma and Aunt Bertha were doing the supper dishes. Sweyn, the big sissy, had left to go sit on the Vinson's front porch and hold hands with his girl, Marie. Papa was reading *The Farm Journal*. Tom was pacing back and forth in the parlor with his hands behind his back. I guess this made Papa nervous.

"What is the matter with you?" he asked as he dropped the magazine into his lap.

Tom stopped pacing and looked at Papa. "Sweyn wants to be a doctor when he grows up, and I want to be a journalist just like you," Tom said.

Papa nodded. "That is what you have both always said."

"Then why don't you let Sweyn start learning how to be a doctor working with Dr. LeRoy and let me help you at the *Advocate*?" Tom asked.

"S.D. couldn't possibly be of any help to Dr. LeRoy now," Papa said. "It takes years to become an intern. But he can help me at the *Advocate*."

"There isn't anything Sweyn can do that I can't do better with my great brain," Tom said. "I could learn how to run the Washington Press and set type twice as fast as he can."

"I'm afraid you aren't old enough," Papa said. "Don't forget that your brother is almost two years older than you."

"I'm not a kid anymore," Tom said as if Papa had insulted him.

"I know how you feel, son," Papa said gently. "You just have growing pains, but you will get over them."

Tom looked as if he'd just lost the ball game. He joined me on the floor where we played checkers until it was bedtime. I knew he didn't have his mind on the game because I beat him two times out of six.

As we got undressed for bed that night, I looked closely at Tom. I couldn't see any difference in him.

"Do they hurt?" I asked.

"Does what hurt?" he asked.

"The growing pains," I said.

Tom folded his britches over the back of his chair. "Some kids grow too fast and that makes their bones and muscles ache," he said. "That is what they call growing pains. But that isn't what Papa meant. He thinks I'm just a kid and too young to help him at the *Advocate* but I'll show him some way that I'm not."

"You must be sick," I said. "You take on any more work and you won't have any time to play."

"When you get as old as me, J.D.," he said shaking his head, "you will understand there are more important things than just playing."

"Boy!" I said. "I hope I never get so old I'd rather work than play, especially during the summer vacation."

Tom's great brain must have been working in his sleep because he was smiling when we got up the next morning. I didn't find out the reason for the smiles until we'd finished breakfast and Papa was having his second cup of coffee.

"Why have you kept that old Ramage Press in that crate in the rear of the *Advocate* office all these years?" Tom asked.

"Sentimental reasons, I guess," Papa answered. "I published my first newspaper in Utah on that press, *The Silverlode Advocate*, when Silverlode was a booming mining town."

"Can I have it?" Tom asked eagerly.

"What in the world would you do with it?" Papa asked.

84

"J.D. and I can clean out a corner in the barn," Tom said quickly. "We could practice being newspapermen."

Papa appeared to be thinking about it for a moment. "The press is just lying there," he finally said, "and the type that goes with it is in the crate. I couldn't use the type when I bought the Washington Press, which uses a larger type."

Mamma helped Papa make up his mind. "Let the boys have it," she said.

"Why not?" Sweyn asked. "Then the little grade-school kids can play at being journalists."

Tom glared at my oldest brother. "I'll make you eat those words someday," he said.

"No quarreling," Mamma said.

Papa smiled. "All right, T.D.," he said. "You can have the Ramage Press."

We moved the Ramage Press to the barn that afternoon. Then Papa showed Tom how to set type in what he called the make-ready. I didn't know why Papa was bothering because Tom had watched him set type many times and probably could have done it blindfolded with his great brain. Than Papa oiled the press and put the make-ready in the bed of the press. He put a card on it and turned the wheel of the press. Then he lifted out the calling card and handed it to Tom. I peeked over my brother's shoulder and read:

T. D. FITZGERALD

"There you are, T.D.," Papa said. "You can start learning to be a journalist by printing calling cards for all your friends."

The next morning after Tom and I had done our chores, he told me to get my wagon and follow him. We went to the

rear of the Z.C.M.I. store. Tom went inside and asked Mr.
Harmon if we could have one of his big wooden packing
crates. Mr. Harmon came to the rear loading platform of the
store. He told us we could take any wooden crate except the
one a dog called Old Butch used for a home. Tom and I
loaded the big wooden box on my wagon. When we got to the
barn, he sent me to the toolshed for a hammer.

"What are you going to do?" I asked.

"Make a desk," he answered.

He finished making himself a desk by noon.

After lunch I followed Tom to the barn, where he prac-
ticed setting type until the kids came by for us to go swimming. Tom said he didn't feel like going. It was a hot afternoon and just right for swimming so I went along.

Tom didn't go swimming with us for the next two days,
staying in the barn working with his press. Then I figured he
got tired of being a journalist because he joined us swimming
and playing until we'd finished delivering the weekly *Advocate* the following Tuesday.

"Take my bike," he said as we returned home, "and go
tell Basil, Sammy, Danny, Seth, and Jimmie Peterson to meet
me in our barn right after lunch."

"What's up?" I asked.

"You'll find out this afternoon," Tom said mysteriously.

I was curious, especially when Tom locked the door from
the inside and wouldn't let any of us in until I told him
everybody was there. Then he unlocked the door from the
inside but told me not to let anybody in until he called to me.

"All right, J.D.," I heard him shout a moment later,
"you can all come in now."

I walked into the barn with the other kids and stood star-

86

ing pop-eyed. Tom was seated behind his desk wearing a green eye shade and an old printer's apron that Papa must have given him. There was a printed sign tacked to a piece of two-by-four on the desk which read:

THE ADENVILLE BUGLE

T. D. FITZGERALD

EDITOR AND PUBLISHER

Laid out on his desk were six printed calling cards, which we all crowded around to read:

THIS IS TO CERTIFY

―――――――――――――

is a reporter for

THE ADENVILLE BUGLE

Then Tom leaned back on his nail keg chair and put his thumbs under his armpits.

"How many of you would like to be reporters for my newspaper?" he asked.

We all raised our hands.

"Do you know what a reporter does?" Tom asked.

Sammy Leeds nodded. "Sure," he said. "A reporter reports the news to his editor."

"Right," Tom said. "A good reporter is one who keeps his eyes and ears open and reports the news whether it is good or bad. But how many of you know what is news and what isn't news?"

It was a tough question because nobody answered.

"I will tell you," Tom said. "If everybody in town knows something, then it isn't news. If only a very few people know something, then it is news to the rest of the people."

Danny Forester shrugged helplessly. "How are we going

to know if only a few people or a lot of people know something?" he asked.

"Easy," Tom said. "If you overhear somebody say to somebody else, 'don't breathe a word of this to anyone,' that is news. If you hear somebody say, 'I wouldn't want this to go any further,' that is news. There are a lot of things in this town only a few people know about. It will be your job as reporters to find out what these are."

"But," Sammy protested and without his sly look on his city-slicker face, "my Pa and Ma never talk about things like that until after I go to bed."

"Then stay awake and sneak down the stairways and listen," Tom said. "The only local news my father prints is what people tell him when they want him to print it. For example, what was the local news in the *Advocate* delivered this morning? Mrs. Hanson left Friday to visit her sister in Provo. Mrs. Leonard entertained the Ladies' Sewing Circle at her home last Thursday. Mr. Phillips was made a deacon in the Church of Jesus Christ of Latter-day Saints. Mrs. Sheldon gave birth to a baby boy last Wednesday night. This isn't real news for my money. By the time the *Advocate* comes out on Tuesday everybody knows it. I don't want this kind of news for the *Bugle*. I want the kind of news that will reveal the deep secrets in this town that the public is entitled to know. Now line up, men, and I'll give you your press cards and assignments."

"Basil, your assignment will be the Palace Cafe your father owns. Strangers in town eat there and what they say may be news to people who live here. Seth, your mother is the biggest gossip in town. It will be your job to report the gossip. Jimmie, your mother runs a boardinghouse, so you listen to what everybody says, and report anything that is news. Danny, your father owns the barbershop and barbers hear a lot of things other people don't know. Your assignment is to find out what these things are. Sammy, your father gets into more arguments than any man in town. It will be your job to report about any of these arguments everybody doesn't know about. J.D., you will cover the Marshal's office and report who is arrested and why."

Then Tom stood up and placed his hands on his desk. "We've got a newspaper to get out by Saturday, men," he said dramatically. "You will all report here Friday afternoon right after lunch to turn in your news stories."

I watched the other reporters swagger out of our barn and then looked at Tom. "I don't think Papa intended for you to get out a real newspaper in competition with his newspaper," I said. "He isn't going to like it."

"I know, J.D.," Tom said, "but it is the only way I can convince Papa that I'm old enough to help him at the *Advocate*."

I left the barn and ran all the way to the Marshal's office. Uncle Mark was sitting in his swivel chair at his rolltop desk. I was disappointed not to see any prisoners in the three cells. I showed him my press card and asked him if there was any news about robberies or murders or cattle rustling.

"I'm afraid not, John," he said. Then he got me to tell him about Tom starting a newspaper in competition with Papa. I didn't think it was funny, but it made Uncle Mark laugh like all get out.

But the next morning Uncle Mark sure wasn't laughing because the Adenville Bank was robbed of more than ten thousand dollars during the night. These robbers didn't ride into town in the daytime and hold up the bank and ride out of town the way outlaws should. If they had, Uncle Mark could have formed a posse and tracked them down. Papa told us during lunch what a dirty trick these robbers had played on my uncle.

Uncle Mark always kept a close watch on the two saloons on the east side of the railroad tracks because that was where fights and trouble usually started. After the saloons closed, he went to bed because everybody else in town was in bed by then. It was while everybody was asleep that the robbers acted.

They entered the home of Calvin Whitlock, the banker, at about two in the morning. They picked a good time because his sister was in Salt Lake City visiting relatives and his housekeeper, Mrs. Hazzleton, went to her own house at night. Mr. Whitlock was a widower who had never remarried and didn't have any children.

Nobody in Adenville locked their doors at night so it was no trick for the robbers to enter the house. They sneaked into the banker's bedroom and woke Mr. Whitlock. They were wearing long yellow rain slickers, had their hats pulled way down on their heads so he couldn't see their hair, and were wearing masks made from red bandana handkerchiefs with holes cut in them so they could see. One of them put a pistol to Mr. Whitlock's head and motioned for him to get out of bed and get dressed. Without speaking a word they marched the banker to the Adenville Bank and made him open the door with his key. Using sign language the robber with the pistol gave Mr. Whitlock the choice of opening the safe or having his brains blown out. Mr. Whitlock decided his life was worth more than the money and opened the safe. The robbers tied him to a chair and put a gag in his mouth. Then they put the money from the safe into an old leather valise and left.

Nobody knew what had happened until Mrs. Hazzleton

90

went to call Mr. Whitlock for breakfast and found the banker's bedroom empty. She telephoned Uncle Mark, who got Frank Collopy, who worked in the bank, to open the front door of the bank. They found Mr. Whitlock still tied to the chair.

"If the robbery isn't solved," Papa said as he finished telling us about it at lunch, "the depositors at the bank will lose their money."

I ran to the Marshal's office after lunch and found Uncle Mark studying wanted posters. I showed him my press card in case he'd forgotten I was a genuine reporter.

"What are you doing?" I asked.

Uncle Mark looked plenty worried. "I thought I might get a lead from some of these wanted posters," he said. "But I can't find a single wanted man who ever pulled off a bank robbery like this one at night."

There was one thing I really liked about Uncle Mark. He never talked down to Tom and me, but treated us just like grownups.

"Maybe they left town right after the robbery," I said, trying to be helpful.

"I wish they had," Uncle Mark said. "That would give me a lead. Horses make tracks. And if they had left town they would have headed for the Nevada line taking the shortcut over the Frisco mountains. But I rode out and checked this morning. There are no fresh tracks turning off the road toward the Nevada line. And I checked out all the drifters and strangers who were in town yesterday. They are all still here."

"If nobody can identify them how can you catch them?" I asked.

"Stolen money always burns a hole in a robber's pocket," Uncle Mark said. "I don't want Tom printing this in his

91

newspaper but I'll just wait until one of them starts spending a lot of money in the saloons drinking and gambling."

"What if they don't?" I asked, trying to be helpful.

"Then I'll just keep an eye on any strangers or drifters who leave town suddenly and get a posse and track them down," Uncle Mark answered.

When I returned home, I found Tom at his desk in the barn. I told him what Uncle Mark had said.

"Uncle Mark is a good peace officer," Tom said, "but he isn't using his head. These robbers are too slick to start spending a lot of money in town and too smart to leave town until things cool off so no suspicion will be attached to them. And I don't believe the robbery was pulled by any drifters or strangers in town."

"Why not?" I asked.

"Because the robbers took too much care in making sure they couldn't be identified," Tom said. "They didn't even speak, which means one of them or maybe both were afraid Mr. Whitlock would recognize their voice."

"Well, they sure aren't Mormons," I said, "because Mormons don't go around robbing banks. And they sure don't live on this side of town because everybody living west of the tracks are law-abiding citizens."

"Good thinking, J.D.," Tom said. "That leaves just somebody living in the Sheepmen's Hotel or the rooming house on the other side of the railroad tracks. Which means they must eat their meals in the Palace Cafe or in the Sheepmen's Hotel restaurant. And that gives me an idea. Go get Basil."

"I no got no news yet," Basil said when we entered the

93

barn. "I sit in corner of cafe and listen to customers for supper last night until eight o'clock but no hear no news."

"I think the men who robbed the bank must eat some of their meals in your father's cafe," Tom said. "As one of my reporters, it will be your job to listen to the customers without letting them know you are listening."

"How I do that?" Basil asked.

"You can hide behind the counter in the dining room where your father keeps his pies and cakes and things," Tom said. "You can listen to what the customers say without them knowing it."

"Maybe Papa don't let me," Basil said.

"Show him your press card and tell him you work for me," Tom said. "Tell him it is a part of being one-hundred-percent American boy."

The next morning after doing my share of the morning chores I went to the Marshal's Office. Uncle Mark wasn't there but there was a prisoner in one of the cells. It was Mr. Haggerty, who got drunk every couple of weeks and disturbed the peace so much that Uncle Mark had to lock him up until he was sober. He was sitting on the bunk in his cell holding his head in his hands. Since it was my duty as a reporter to interview all prisoners, I walked to the door of the cell.

"Mr. Haggerty, why do you get drunk?" I asked.

He raised his head and looked at me with bloodshot eyes. "It's that wife of mine, sonny," he said. "She nags and nags at me until I have to get drunk or go out of my mind."

I figured this was news because nobody but me and Mr. Haggerty knew why he got drunk. I made a note of it in my reporter's notebook.

Friday afternoon right after lunch all the reporters arrived at our barn to turn in their reports. Tom sat behind his desk with his green eye shade over his eyes. He had a pencil in his hand and a big notebook on his desk. He asked me to report first. I told him what Mr. Haggerty had told me.

"Very good, J.D.," Tom said as he wrote in his notebook. "That is news. I've often wondered why he got drunk."

One by one Sammy, Seth, Danny, and Jimmie made their reports. All of them had one or more items that Tom considered newsworthy enough to write in his notebook.

"You're next, Basil," he said.

"I wait until other reporters leave," Basil said.

"Some reporter," Sammy said with a sneer. "He didn't get any news."

Tom had an excited look on his face as he ordered the other reporters to leave. When all of them had left the barn, he looked at Basil.

"You found out something about the robbery?" he asked with excitement.

"I know who rob bank," Basil said proudly. "I no want to say in front of other reporters. Afraid maybe they tell before *Bugle* is published."

"Wow!" Tom shouted. "What a story!" Then he gripped his pencil. "Let's have it, Basil."

Basil told us he was pretty downhearted by Thursday evening because he hadn't heard anything from customers at the cafe that sounded like news. He asked his father if he could stay up hiding behind the counter until the cafe closed at nine o'clock. At first his father said no, but when Basil explained he would lose his job as a reporter on the *Bugle* if he didn't get some news, his father agreed.

At eight-thirty two customers entered the cafe for a late

supper. They sat down at a table and ordered steaks smothered in onions and hash-brown potatoes, apple pie, and coffee. Mr. Kokovinis went into the kitchen to prepare the meal. Basil's mother was in the apartment where they lived above the cafe. Basil took a chance and peeked around the corner of the counter. He recognized Hank Williams, who had been working in the livery stable since coming to town about three months ago. He was a regular customer at the cafe. The other man was Frank Jackson, who had also been a regular customer in the cafe since coming to town a couple of weeks ago. His father had told him that Jackson was a gambler. Basil was about to give up when he heard the men begin to quarrel about the robbery.

"I say, let's take the loot and blow town," Jackson said.

"Keep your voice down," Williams said.

"The Greek is in the kitchen and can't hear us," Jackson said.

"We made a bargain when I sent for you," Williams said. "If we pull out right away, the Marshal will put two and two together and be right on our tail with a posse. But if we just stick it out for a month and then pull out, it won't attract any suspicion. We pulled off a perfect robbery, and if we just stick to our bargain we can never be arrested for it."

"I guess you're right," Jackson said. "But are you sure nobody will find that valise in the livery stable?"

"I've got it well hidden under some hay," Williams said.

Basil remained behind the counter until the men had eaten and left the cafe.

"Did you tell your father?" Tom asked as Basil finished his story.

"No," Basil answered. "Afraid Papa want to tell Marshal."

96

I was so excited I was trembling. "I'll go get Uncle Mark!" I shouted.

"You will do no such thing," Tom said. "And you will give me your word you won't breathe a word of this to anybody."

"But you must tell Uncle Mark," I said.

"We will tell him, but not until just before the first edition of the *Bugle* hits the streets tomorrow," Tom said. He dropped his pencil on the desk and began rubbing his hands. "Boy, am I going to scoop Papa's newspaper. He'll wish he'd never said I was too young to help him at the *Advocate*. I'll start setting the type for the first edition of the *Bugle* right now. You will have to do my chores this afternoon."

"Why should I?" I asked.

"Because I can set type and you can't, and we've got a newspaper to get out," Tom answered. Then he looked at Basil. "You've done a great job of reporting," he said. "I will see you get full credit for it in the *Bugle*. Now go tell all the other reporters I want them here at nine o'clock tomorrow morning, but don't mention anything about the robbery being solved."

I not only got stuck doing Tom's chores and mine that afternoon but also the next morning. Tom said he'd found some typographical errors in the type he had set and wanted to correct them.

"I can't slug the type to make the columns come out even," he told me right after breakfast, "because I haven't enough experience yet. But I can make sure there are no typographical errors."

All the reporters arrived at nine o'clock just as I finished the chores. We all went into the barn. Tom had two pairs of old scissors Mamma had given him. He put Sammy and Danny to work cutting strips of newsprint 7½ inches by 10 inches. We had to wait until they had a hundred sheets cut.

"We are ready to roll, men," Tom said. "I'll turn the wheel of the press and ink the make-ready. J.D., you feed the sheets into the press. Basil, you pull out the printed copies. The rest of you lay the printed copies on bales of hay and around the barn so the ink can dry."

As the first copy of the *Bugle* came off the press, and Basil handed it to Sammy, I heard Sammy yell, "Holy Toledo, we solved the bank robbery!"

It was just like Sammy to take some of the credit and make such a commotion we had to stop the press while we all crowded around the bale of hay where the first copy lay drying. I couldn't help swelling up with pride as I read the one-page first edition of the *Bugle*.

THE ADENVILLE BUGLE
READ IT FIRST IN THE *Bugle*

T. D. Fitzgerald
Editor and Publisher

Vol. 1
Price One Cent

THE *BUGLE* SOLVES
BANK ROBBERY

Acting upon information furnished by the *Bugle,* Marshal Mark Trainor arrested Hank Williams and Frank Jackson for the robbery of the Adenville Bank just a few minutes before this first edition of the *Bugle* was released to the public. All the stolen money was recovered from under some hay in the livery stable, where Williams has worked for about three months since coming to town.

LOCAL NEWS OF INTEREST

If Mrs. Haggerty will stop nagging her husband all the time, he will stop getting drunk. Sarah Pickens is going to die an old maid because she is too stuck up and choosey to marry a local man who loves her. The Winters' dog, Bess, had pups. Anybody wanting a pup see Mr. or Mrs. Winters. Robert Bates got stung on the horse he bought from Steve Andrews because the horse is windbroken. If the

The robbery was solved by the great detective work of Basil Kokovinis, a *Bugle* reporter, and the great brain of the Editor and Publisher of this newspaper.

The Editor and Publisher of the *Bugle* deduced the robbers were from the east side of the railroad tracks and must eat some of their meals in The Palace Cafe. He assigned his reporter to hide behind the counter in the cafe and listen for anything suspicious customers might say.

At eight-thirty Thursday evening Williams and Jackson entered the cafe to eat supper. They placed their order with Mr. Kokovinis, the proprietor, who went into the kitchen to prepare the meal. Then the two robbers began to quarrel about the robbery, with Jackson wanting to take the loot and leave town at once and Williams insisting they remain in town for a month before leaving so as not to attract any suspicion to them. The *Bugle* reporter hidden behind the counter heard every word.

The citizens of Adenville can thank the *Bugle* for solving what would have otherwise been a perfect crime. And remember, you always read it first in the *Bugle*.

Widow Rankin spent as much money on her kids as she does on herself trying to catch a new husband, her kids wouldn't look like ragamuffins. Mrs. Lee's brother, Stanley, isn't in the Army like she tells people. He is serving time in the State Penitentiary. Anybody wanting a kitten see Mrs. Carter. Dan Thomas had better find a job soon or his brother-in-law, Mr. Forester, is going to throw Dan out on his ear. The kids in town made a deal with Mr. Smith. They are going to keep all the weeds cleared from the Smith vacant lot in return for using it as a playground.

EDITORIAL

Some parents don't seem to realize that their kids are growing up and continue to treat them like little kids. When a boy gets to be eleven going on twelve, his parents should start treating him like a young man and not like a kid anymore.

All the reporters were as excited as all get out after reading the first edition of the *Bugle* and anxious to start selling it. But we had to wait until we'd printed the rest of the hundred copies and then wait for them to dry.

Then Tom handed me a copy. "You and Basil take this

to Uncle Mark," he said. "Stay with him until he has the bank robbers in jail. Then let me know so I can turn my other reporters loose selling the *Bugle* to the public."

Basil and I ran to the Marshal's Office. Uncle Mark was sitting in his swivel chair. I thrust a copy of the *Bugle* in his hands.

Uncle Mark jumped to his feet while still reading.

"Tom wants you to make the arrests quietly so nobody knows until they read it in the *Bugle*," I said.

"Will do," Uncle Mark said with a grin. Then he looked at Basil. "Thanks, Basil, and be sure you thank Tom for me. I'll take Hank Williams first."

"As reporters, we've got to see the arrest," I said.

"All right, boys," Uncle Mark said, "but just act natural. Follow me to the livery stable. I'll go in the front but bring Williams out the back way."

Basil and I were in the alley behind the livery stable when Uncle Mark came out the back way with Hank Williams and carrying a leather valise. He walked Williams up alleys as if they were just taking a friendly walk and got the man locked up in a cell without anybody noticing.

Then Uncle Mark opened the valise and looked at the money before he locked it up in his rolltop desk.

"I've got you cold, Hank," he said to the prisoner. "Take my advice and confess and plead guilty and it will go easier for you."

"What can I do but confess and plead guilty?" Williams asked sadly. "You knew where the loot was hidden and everything. Jackson must have told you." Then he got a startled look on his face. "Where is Frank?"

"I'm on my way to arrest him now," Uncle Mark said.

Basil and I followed Uncle Mark to the Sheepmen's Hotel.

Jackson must have been in bed because it seemed like a long time before Uncle Mark came out of the rear of the hotel with the prisoner. Basil and I walked close enough to hear as Uncle Mark walked Jackson up the alley.

"You might as well confess and plead guilty," Uncle Mark said. "I've got Hank Williams locked up and the money from the robbery. Hank confessed and is going to plead guilty."

Jackson shrugged. "If that is the case, what else can I do?" he said.

Basil and I followed all the way up alleys and to the jail without anybody noticing anything. Uncle Mark locked Jackson in the cell next to Williams. Then he looked at Basil and me.

"You can go tell Tom he can start selling his newspaper now," he said.

Basil ran out of the jail but I stayed.

"You squealer!" Jackson shouted at Williams.

"I didn't squeal," Williams said. "I thought you did."

"I sure didn't," Jackson said.

Hank Williams pushed his face between the bars of his cell. "How did you ever figure it, Marshal?" he pleaded.

"I didn't," Uncle Mark said as he took the copy of the *Bugle* from his pocket and handed it to Williams.

"The boy who is the editor and publisher of this newspaper and his reporter solved the robbery."

I never in my life saw such a flabbergasted look on a robber's face as Williams read the story in the *Bugle*.

"I wouldn't have minded so much, Marshal," he said as if he wanted to cry, "if it had been you. But a couple of kids.

The boys at the State Pen will ride Frank and me plenty for this."

"What is going on?" Jackson hollered from his cell.

"Don't tell him, Marshal," Williams pleaded. "It will make him cry."

Uncle Mark passed the copy of the *Bugle* to Jackson. Then we heard a lot of commotion in the street. I ran outside with Uncle Mark. I could see our reporters waving copies of the *Bugle* in the air on every corner on Main Street. I could hear them shouting: "Bank robbery solved! Read all about it in the *Bugle*! A penny a copy!"

And boy, oh boy, were they doing a land-office business. People were running out of stores and out of their homes and buying up copies of the *Bugle* like I'd never seen anybody buy anything in my life. But it was strange how people standing on Main Street reading the *Bugle* were acting. Some of the men were slapping each other on the back. Some of the men and women were reading and just staring as if they couldn't believe the robbery had been solved. Some were laughing, while others looked positively angry.

I felt Uncle Mark's hand on my shoulder. "I'd better take the stolen money back to the bank now," he said.

I ran back to the barn to tell Tom that the first edition of the *Bugle* was a big success. I found my brother sitting behind his desk with his green eye shade pushed up on his forehead and his thumbs hooked under his armpits.

"You did it, T.D.!" I shouted. "People are buying the *Bugle* like they never bought the *Advocate*. You proved to Papa you are old enough and smart enough to be a journalist."

Tom nodded modestly. "Papa has often told us about the wars between rival newspapers in Utah," he said. "If he doesn't give me a job on the *Advocate* now, it will be war

102

between the *Bugle* and the *Advocate*. And I'll scoop him every week."

Just then Sammy, Danny, and Jimmie came running into the barn. They told Tom they were sold out.

"We'll print another hundred copies," Tom said. "J.D., you run down to the *Advocate* office and tell Papa I'll need some more newsprint."

I ran all the way to the *Advocate* office but didn't go inside because I couldn't. There was a big crowd on the wooden sidewalk and in the street in front of the office. Papa was standing in the doorway looking as if he wished he was on a deserted island. He was holding a copy of the *Bugle* in his hand. I couldn't blame Papa for the way he looked. Tom had really scooped him good.

And you never saw such a commotion. Mrs. Haggerty was shouting insults at Papa. Sarah Pickens was crying. Mrs. Lee was hysterical, with two other women trying to quiet her down. The Widow Rankin was screaming she was going to sue Papa. Mr. Bates and Steve Andrews were fighting. Danny's father, Mr. Forester, and his brother-in-law, Dan Thomas, were taking off their coats and getting ready to fight. The rest of the crowd were laughing like it was all a big joke.

Then Uncle Mark, who must have just returned from the bank where he'd taken the stolen money, pushed his way through the crowd to Papa's side. He took out his Colt .45 and fired a couple of shots in the air. Everybody shut up and stared at him.

"You men stop that fighting and arguing and you women stop that shouting and crying or I'll throw all of you in jail for disturbing the peace," Uncle Mark said.

Everybody in town knew Uncle Mark never made idle threats. The fighting stopped and there was complete silence.

103

"If any of you have complaints to make," Uncle Mark said, "you will act like law-abiding citizens and come to my office and sign a complaint. If any of you think you have grounds for a libel suit, you will consult your attorney and act on his advice. I will not tolerate a mob. Now break up this crowd and go about your business."

"Just a moment," Papa said. "I have something I would like to say. I cannot condone what my son has done and assure you who are concerned that he will be severely punished. But the fact remains that he and Basil Kokovinis did solve the bank robbery. If it had not been for these two boys, many of you who are depositors at the bank would have lost your money."

That made the crowd think, as many began to nod their heads. Then Papa held up a copy of the *Bugle*.

"As for the local news column," he said, "none of it is really news except for the pups the Winters' family have to give away, and the kittens the Carters have to give away, and the item about the boys in town clearing the weeds from the Smiths' vacant lot. Nothing else in this local news column is news because they are things that people in this town have known about for some time. All my son has done is to bring out into the open what has been said over backyard fences. I admit it was a cruel thing to do, and in very bad taste, but he is only a boy and didn't know any better. I apologize to each of you for what he has done and will make him apologize to each of you. Thank you for listening to me."

The crowd broke up, but Papa looked to be as angry as a burro with a cocklebur under his pack saddle. He walked so swiftly toward our house that I had to run to keep up with him. He didn't slow down or stop until he entered our barn, where Tom and the reporters were waiting.

"Where is the newsprint?" Tom asked as if surprised.

"I'll newsprint you," Papa said, and I thought from the way he said it that Tom was due for the first whipping of his life. Then Papa sort of swallowed a couple of times. "Ask your friends to leave," he said.

All the reporters left except me.

Tom leaned back on his nail keg chair and pushed his green eye shade up on his forehead. "What is the idea?" he asked as if just curious and not scared at all.

Papa's face turned red and his cheeks puffed up like a squirrel with a jawful of nuts. He sat down on a bale of hay. Finally he spoke.

"You have caused your mother and me more anguish and embarrassment in one day than all the kids in town put together could cause their parents in a year," Papa said.

To my astonishment Tom grinned. "Are you sure you aren't just upset because I scooped the *Advocate,* Papa?" he asked.

"Solving the bank robbery was good journalism," Papa admitted. "You and Basil did the community, and especially the depositors at the bank, a great service."

Tom nodded wisely. "I guess that proves I'm old enough to learn how to run the Washington Press and help you at the *Advocate,*" he said.

"I haven't finished yet," Papa said. "Your local news column except for three items wasn't news fit to print. In the first place it wasn't news at all because every adult in town already knew about the Haggertys, Sarah Pickens, Mrs. Lee's brother, and all the rest of it. In the second place it was a type of journalism that feeds on scandal, that hurts people, and is in very bad taste."

Papa paused for a moment to let this sink in. "A good

105

journalist doesn't deliberately hurt people just to sell newspapers," he said. "It is true a good newspaperman seeks to expose evil when that evil is a threat to the community. If a public official is corrupt, it is the duty of a newspaper editor to expose that official as being corrupt, because a newspaper is thereby performing a good service for the community. But when you print that Mrs. Haggerty's nagging drives her husband to drink, and all the other scandal in your local news column, that is an invasion of their privacy and subject to libel laws. Moreover, it performs no useful service for the community. Your mother and I do quarrel on occasions as you are well aware. It is a part of married life. But how would you like it if somebody printed in a newspaper that your mother and I were fighting like cats and dogs all the time?"

I'd never seen Tom's face so dejected as he bit his lower lip. "I was only trying to prove to you that I wasn't just a kid anymore," he said in a whisper. "I didn't mean to hurt anybody."

"I got the message in your editorial," Papa said. "But the only thing you proved to me was that you are too young to do anything for me at the *Advocate* except to deliver it."

Then Papa stood up. "You have done a terrible thing and must be punished for it," he said. "You will never have the opportunity to publish another edition of the *Bugle*. I'm going to have the Ramage Press and type crated and taken back to the *Advocate* office. That will be only part of your punishment. You will do your chores without any allowance for the next four weeks and your mother and I will impose the silent treatment for the same period of time. And tomorrow, you will go around and personally apologize to everybody slandered in the *Bugle*."

I sure felt sorry for Tom but guess I must have looked

sort of relieved because I wasn't included in the punishment.

"Wipe that smirk off your face, J.D.," Papa said. "For your part in this, you are also included in the silent treatment."

"But Papa——" I started to protest I was an innocent victim but he just walked out of the barn. The silent treatment had begun.

I looked at Tom. "Your great brain sure got us into a mess this time," I said, putting the blame where I felt it belonged.

"Beat it, J.D.," he said. "I want to be alone."

I left the barn and shut the door. I walked part way across our corral and then sneaked back and peeked into the barn through a knothole. I couldn't believe my eyes. Tom sat at his desk with his head cradled in his arms, and his shoulders were shaking. Even outside the barn I could hear the muffled sobs coming from his throat. The Great Brain was crying! I couldn't ever remember seeing him cry before. Even when he fell one time while we were playing follow-the-leader and had broken his arm, he didn't cry.

CHAPTER FIVE

The Death of Old Butch

IT WAS JUST A COUPLE OF WEEKS after I'd seen
Tom cry for the first time that a dog named Old Butch died.
He was a mongrel dog, who was everybody's dog, and yet he
was nobody's dog. I know that sounds funny, but it is true.
He had big ears like a hound dog, a squat body like a bulldog,
and only the good Lord knows how many other breeds were
in his ancestry. He was mostly black and brown with white
spots.

Nobody knew where Old Butch came from. Mr. Harmon,
who ran the Z.C.M.I. store, believed the dog was left behind
accidently by some people passing through town. Maybe he
was right because Old Butch made his home in a packing case

behind the store, and sometimes he'd sit for hours is front of the store as if waiting for the people to come back for him.

Some of those people must have been kids because Old Butch really loved kids. He was like a godsend to every kid in town whose parents wouldn't let them own a dog. He'd play with them and let them pretend he was their dog whenever they wanted. And there are times when a boy really needs a dog. I know when I was getting the silent treatment, there were many times when I went down behind the barn to cry, and my dog Brownie was always there to comfort me. He'd lick the tears from my face and let me hug him while he comforted me. And I knew a lot of kids in town who didn't have a dog who would head straight for Old Butch after getting a whipping. Old Butch would lick their faces and comfort them.

Grownups liked Old Butch too. They would stop and pat him on the head whenever they met him. But he just wouldn't let anybody really own him. He made his rounds every day. He'd stop in front of the Deseret Meat Market first. He didn't beg. He'd just sit on the wooden sidewalk until Mr. Thompson came out and gave him a bone or some scraps. And he would go behind the Palace Cafe and sit until Mr. Kokovinis brought him some scraps. And the kids who didn't own a dog would sneak food out of their homes for Old Butch. He was probably the best fed dog in town.

Plenty of kids tried to make him their dog and took him home with them. Some even built a doghouse for him. But he would only stay for a day or so and then go back to his packing-case home.

Tom and I had just finished doing our morning chores the day Roger Gillis came running into our backyard. He was a kid about six years old whose parents wouldn't let him own a dog. He was crying.

"Old Butch is dead!" he cried. "I went to look for him to play with this morning and found him dead."

"He was getting pretty old for a dog," Tom said, trying to comfort Roger.

That was sure true. I could remember Old Butch from the time I was very little. Nobody knew who named him Butch, and then as he got old everybody started calling him Old Butch.

"Maybe he isn't really dead," Tom said. "Maybe he is just sick."

"He looks dead," Roger said.

"Stop crying until we make sure," Tom said.

My brother went up to our bedroom and got a small pocket mirror from his strongbox. The three of us ran all the way to the rear of the Z.C.M.I. store.

Old Butch lay on a blanket some kid had put in the crate a long time ago. His eyes were open and he looked all stiff.

Tom knelt and held the mirror in front of Old Butch's nose and mouth. The mirror remained dry and bright. Tom stood up and put the mirror in his pocket.

"He is dead all right," Tom said.

Bad news travels fast in a small town. Andy Anderson and Howard Kay and Jimmie Peterson and Seth Smith came running up the alley. They were all kids whose mothers wouldn't let them have a dog. Their mothers said dogs made too much of a mess on the lawns and gardens.

Then Uncle Mark came riding up the alley on his white stallion. He stopped and dismounted. He took his lariat from his saddle and started making a noose on one end.

"What are you going to do?" Tom asked.

110

"Mr. Harmon reported finding the dog dead," Uncle Mark said. "It is my duty as Marshal to get rid of the body. I'll drag him out of town a mile or so."

Tom folded his arms on his chest. "You aren't going to drag Old Butch out of town and leave him for the buzzards," he said.

"There isn't anything else I can do," Uncle Mark said. "He is just a dog, and he is dead."

"He was more than just a dog," Tom said. "Maybe you can't do anything about it, but us kids can."

"Like what?" Uncle Mark asked with a surprised look.

"Like giving Old Butch the proper funeral he deserves," Tom said. "All the kids in town loved Old Butch, and we aren't going to let the buzzards have his body."

"All right, boys," Uncle Mark said, "but you'll have to bury him today."

Tom became all business as soon as Uncle Mark rode away. "J.D., get your wagon," he said. "Seth, you go get Sammy, Danny, and Basil and meet us in our barn. Jimmie, go into the store and tell Mr. Harmon we are going to take a small wooden box with boards pried up on top to make a coffin for Old Butch."

By the time I returned with my wagon, there were a whole bunch of kids there. Old Butch's body, wrapped in the blanket, lay in a smaller wooden box than the crate that had been his home. Tom and I lifted the box onto my wagon.

When we arrived at our barn, Seth, Sammy, Danny, and Basil were waiting.

"Sammy," Tom said, "you and Danny and Basil get shovels out of our toolshed and go dig a grave for Old Butch. Take a pick along too. You might need it."

They didn't ask questions. They all knew there was a

small piece of ground just south of the cemetery where people sometimes buried their pets. They left to dig the grave.

"Jimmie," Tom said. "You go to the meat market and tell Mr. Thompson we want a big bone to bury with Old Butch."

Jimmie hitched up his britches, which were too big for him, as he looked at Tom with surprise. "If he is dead, he can't eat," he said.

"The Indians always bury their dead with enough food to last until they get to the happy hunting ground," Tom said. "Maybe there is a happy hunting ground for good dogs like Old Butch. We'll put a bone in his coffin to last him until he gets there."

Tom told me to go ask Mamma if we could have the old American flag she had put in our attic when Papa bought a new one.

I ran to our kitchen, where Mamma and Aunt Bertha were kneading dough to make bread.

"T.D. wants the old flag you put in the attic," I said.

"Why?" Mamma asked.

"To put on the coffin," I said.

"Coffin?" she asked. "Is Mr. Peters dead?"

I guess Mamma thought because Mr. Peters was a Civil War veteran and entitled to have a flag on his coffin that Mr. Peters had died.

"No," I said. "It is Old Butch and I guess Tom wants to give him a military funeral."

"God love that boy," Mamma said. "Sometimes I get so exasperated with him I could scream, and then he does something that makes me very proud he is my son. Of course he can have the old flag."

Mamma wiped the flour from her hands and went up to

the attic to get the flag for me because she couldn't quite remember where she put it. When I returned to the barn with it, Sammy, Danny, and Basil were back from digging the grave. The coffin was on my wagon. Tom draped the flag over it.

"We will let Old Butch lie in state until two o'clock this afternoon," he said.

"But," Sammy said, "only people lie in state."

I couldn't keep my mouth shut I was so curious.

"What is lying in state?" I asked.

"When a person dies," Tom explained, "if he or she has been a good person who is loved and respected, the body in the coffin lies in state in an undertaking parlor, or in the Mormon Tabernacle, or in the Community Church, so people can pay their last respects to the dead. You've seen it, J.D."

"But I didn't know what they called it," I said. "Then Sammy is right. Only people lie in state."

Tom looked angry for a second and then his face became calm. "If that was Brownie lying in that coffin, you'd want him to lie in state, wouldn't you?"

It wasn't until that moment I really understood what Tom was trying to do. There were at least seven or eight kids in the barn right then who felt about Old Butch the same way I did about Brownie.

"You are right," I said. "Old Butch deserves to lie in state."

Tom sat down on a bale of hay. "Now about the funeral procession," he said. "The kids who don't own dogs will be the pallbearers. Basil, you and J.D. will pull the wagon. I mean the hearse. Following the hearse will come the band and after the band the mourners."

We all stared at Tom as if he'd gone loco. The only band in town was the town band made up of grownups.

113

"Sammy," Tom continued, "you will play your cornet in the band and also play 'Taps' at the final resting place."

"I can play 'Taps'," Sammy said, "but I don't know how to play a funeral march."

"I know," Tom said, "so you and the band will play 'Home Sweet Home' instead. You can play that, can't you?"

"It's about the first thing you learn how to play on any instrument," Sammy said.

"Danny will play his trombone," Tom said. "Seth will play his violin. Jimmie will play his clarinet. Howard will play his snare drum, and I will play his bass drum."

Seth shook his head. "Whoever heard of a violin in a band?" he asked. "And besides, you don't know how to play a bass drum."

"You can play 'Home Sweet Home' and that is all that matters," Tom said. "And with my great brain I can learn to beat time on a bass drum in a minute." Tom got up from the bale of hay. "The fellows in the band be here at one-thirty so we can have a rehearsal."

It was time by then for us all to go have lunch.

"We can't leave Old Butch alone," Tom said after the others had left. "I'll stand as honor guard while you eat, and then you can come back and relieve me while I eat."

That was all right with me because it gave me a chance to be in the spotlight during lunch for a change. Papa, Mamma, and Aunt Bertha listened intently as I told them about the funeral arrangements. Sweyn didn't seem impressed at all.

"Whoever heard of a funeral procession for a dog," he said. "It is ridiculous."

Papa glared at Sweyn. "The death of any living thing, be it a plant or an animal or a person is never ridiculous," he

114

said. "You will march in that funeral procession with your brothers."

"At my age?" Sweyn asked with a startled look. "Marie Vinson will think I've gone crazy."

"That isn't what she will think," Papa said. "It is just what you think, and I don't like your thinking at all."

It was almost worth Old Butch dying to see Papa put Sweyn in his place for a change. After I'd eaten, I ran to the barn to tell Tom the good news about how Papa had really told off Sweyn.

"It's about time," Tom said "Sweyn is getting too big for his britches. Now, J.D., stand as honor guard. Any mourners that come before I get back, let them pat the coffin and say good-bye to Old Butch."

In a little while kids started coming into the barn from all over town to say good-bye to Old Butch. Then they stood in small groups, talking in whispers like people do at funerals. The band and everybody were there when Tom got back.

Tom began rehearsing the band. It sounded so bad at first that our cow began to moo, our team became restless, and Dusty began to neigh. But the band finally got so it didn't sound half bad. It was time for the funeral procession to begin.

Basil and I pulled the hearse to the alley. Tom lined up the band behind us. The mourners fell in line, including Sweyn, who looked as if he wished he could find a hole and crawl into it. Tom gave the signal and the band started playing "Home Sweet Home" as the procession began to move up the alley. Following Tom's instructions Basil and I turned when we got to Main Street and led the way right down the middle of Main Street, with the band playing "Home Sweet Home" over and over again.

I could see people coming out of stores and homes and

115

people on the sidewalk staring at us. Then I saw Papa come out of the *Advocate* office. I thought some of the grownups might laugh and think it ridiculous like Sweyn. But they didn't. When we got to the railroad tracks, I looked over my shoulder. Papa and about a hundred adults had joined the funeral procession. You would have thought we were burying the Mayor.

When we reached the grave site and stopped, the pall-bearers placed the coffin in the grave. The band stopped playing. Then Tom stood beside the open grave and I'd never seen his face so solemn.

"I will now deliver the eulogy for Old Butch," he said. "If ever there lived a good dog, it was Old Butch. He loved everybody, and everybody loved him. We are all going to miss Old Butch. But those who will miss him the most are kids whose parents won't let them own a dog of their own. Old Butch took the place of the dogs they couldn't have. And now that Old Butch is gone, these kids are going to be mighty brokenhearted. What these parents don't realize is that a dog is a boy's first great love except for his family. A family without a dog is like a house that is empty." Tom stooped over and picked up a handful of dirt which he sprinkled on the coffin in the grave. " 'Dust thou art and to dust thou return'," he quoted. Then he nodded at Sammy.

Sammy put his cornet to his mouth and began to play "Taps". He played so beautifully it made me cry. But I wasn't the only one crying.

When Sammy finished blowing "Taps" for Old Butch, Seth and Basil picked up the shovels they had left there and began throwing dirt on the coffin. I thought the grownups would leave then, but they didn't. They stayed until the last

116

shovelful of dirt had been placed on the grave. Then they began to leave.

Uncle Mark and Papa walked to where Tom was standing.

"Thanks, Tom," Uncle Mark said, and his voice was hoarse.

Papa put his hand on Tom's shoulder. "I am going to give Old Butch an obituary in the *Advocate*," he said. "And I'm going to let you write it just as you said it here today. Even in death Old Butch is going to make some boys happy. Mr. Gillis told me after hearing your eulogy that he is going to find a pup for his son, Roger. And there are others who heard your eulogy or who will read the obituary in the *Advocate* who will change their minds about their sons owning a dog. I'm proud of you, son."

CHAPTER SIX

The Ghost of Silverlode

JUST THE OTHER SIDE of the town limits of Adenville on the old road leading up Red Rock Canyon lay the
ruins of the ghost town of Silverlode. It had been a booming
silver-mining camp before I was born. Ever since I could remember, there had been a wood sign just this side of Aden
irrigation ditch, which had separated Adenville from the mining camp. The sign read:

> NO PERSON UNDER 18 YEARS OF AGE
> ADMITTED BEYOND THIS SIGN UNLESS
> ACCOMPANIED BY ADULTS BY ORDER
> OF MARSHAL AND DEPUTY SHERIFF
> MARK TRAINOR

119

The road up Red Rock Canyon had been the only road to Silverlode and Adenville until the mines petered out and Silverlode had become a ghost town. Then the railroad had come to Adenville, and a new road had been built that ran northward, following the railroad. The old road up Red Rock Canyon was only used by trappers and hunters. There were so many rock slides and washouts it was impossible to travel by wagon.

I learned when quite young why Uncle Mark had put up the sign. When I was about three years old, two Mormon kids, Larry Knudson and William Bartell, had gone exploring in the ghost town and were never seen again. The ghost town was honeycombed with old mine tunnels and mine shafts and giant excavations. Uncle Mark organized a search party, but a cloudburst that afternoon had washed away all tracks left by the two boys, and the heavy rain had caused landslides, rock slides, and cave-ins. Every able-bodied man in Adenville had searched for the bodies of the two boys for two weeks without success, and then the search was given up.

That was the reason Uncle Mark had put up the sign. But he really didn't need a sign to keep the kids in Adenville from exploring in the ghost town because it was haunted by the ghost of Silverlode. Trappers and hunters returning at night had reported seeing the ghost. Many fathers told their sons they had seen the ghost. And even Uncle Mark said he'd seen the ghost. I remember asking Papa about the ghost when I first heard about it from some other kids.

"They say it is the ghost of a man named Tinker, who owned the Tinker Mine," Papa had told me. "Like other greedy mine owners he refused to put proper safety devices in his mine. The day before the mine closed, six miners were killed when trapped by a cave-in. The miners who escaped

120

lynched Tinker before the Marshal could prevent it. And the miners who lynched Tinker put a curse on him, that he would never know peace in death and would haunt Silverlode forever. They say his ghost comes up from his grave at night and roams the ghost town."

"Have you ever seen the ghost?" I asked.

"No, J.D.," Papa had answered. "But even without a ghost, Silverlode is no place for you or your brothers unless I am with you. What happened to Larry Knudson and William Bartell could happen to any boy foolish enough to go exploring there."

I sure as heck wasn't going to take a chance of being buried alive or meeting up with a ghost. The ghost was welcome to his ghost town as far as every kid in Adenville was concerned until just a couple of weeks before my brothers were to leave for school in Salt Lake City.

It started on a Saturday afternoon. It was raining too hard to go swimming. Some of the kids came to our barn to play, as they often did when it was raining. Seth Smith showed up with his eyes all red.

"Are you sick?" Tom asked as Danny Forester, Sammy Leeds, Parley Benson, Basil, and I crowded around him.

"I didn't sleep all night," Seth said. "My Uncle Steve is visiting us and he likes to tell ghost stories. He was telling us some last night before I went to bed. I was so scared I was afraid to close my eyes all night."

"There is no such thing as a ghost," Tom said.

Sammy looked at my brother as if Tom had just said there was no sun in the sky. "How about the ghost of Silverlode?" he asked. "My own Pa told me he'd seen the ghost."

"And mine," Danny said.

"My Pa too," Seth said.

121

"I don't care what your fathers think they saw," Tom said. "There is no such thing as a ghost."

Sammy got angry. "Are you calling my Pa a liar?" he demanded.

"I'm not calling any of your fathers a liar," Tom said. "All I'm saying is there is no such thing as a ghost, and there is a perfectly logical explanation for what they think they saw."

"But," I protested, "Uncle Mark says he saw the ghost, and he is a Marshal and Deputy Sheriff."

Tom could sure be stubborn at times. "I don't care what Uncle Mark or anybody says. My great brain tells me there is no such thing as a ghost."

Sammy got that sly city-slicker look on his face. "Have you ever been to Silverlode at night?" he asked.

"No," Tom admitted, "but my father took me and my brothers there in the daytime once."

"Everybody knows that ghosts only appear at night," Sammy said. "My Pa says when it gets dark the ghost of Tinker comes right up from his grave. I'll bet you are afraid to go there at night."

"I promised my father I'd never go to Silverlode unless he was with me," Tom said. "And besides, I also promised him I'd never make any more bets with you kids."

"A poor excuse is better than none," Sammy said with a sneering look.

That got to Tom. "If I went there alone at night and came back and told you kids there was no ghost who would believe me?" he asked. "The only way I could prove it would be to have witnesses. All right, Sammy, are you willing to go there at night with me and be a witness?"

Poor old Sammy suddenly lost his sly look. "Why me?" he asked.

"The more witnesses the better," Tom said. "All of you meet me here after curfew Monday night, and I'll prove there is no such thing as the ghost of Silverlode."

I figured Tom had neatly turned the tables on Sammy. None of the kids in their right minds would meet him. But I was wrong.

Parley Benson pushed his coon-skin cap to the back of his head. He patted the Bowie knife in the scabbard on his belt. "I'm not afraid," he said. "I'll meet you."

Tom looked at Parley with surprise but only for a second. "How about you other fellows?" he asked. "The more witnesses the better."

The other kids either had to volunteer or admit they were cowards.

"I'll be here," Sammy said but sure didn't look pleased with the idea.

"Me too," Danny said.

"I'm game if the rest of you are," Seth said and sounded as if he were pronouncing his own death sentence.

"Me no afraid to go," Basil said, "but I can't sneak out of my room."

Basil was right. He lived in an apartment above the Palace Cafe. Even if he jumped from the second-story window of his bedroom and didn't hurt himself, he could never get back in his room.

Tom looked at the rope ladder leading up to his loft. "You can borrow my rope ladder," he said. "Tie it to your bed or something and use it to get out and back into your bedroom."

On Monday morning Papa told Tom and me to come to

123

the *Advocate* office after we'd finished our morning chores and distribute some handbills for a livestock auction.

When we arrived at the *Advocate* office, Tom took one stack of handbills and put them in the basket on his bicycle to deliver in town. I took the other stack with the tack hammer and box of tacks to post on trees and on the light poles on Main Street. I met Seth Smith when I was about half done. He offered to help me.

"I told my Uncle Steve we are going to Silverlode to-night," Seth said.

"Why did you do that?" I asked. "Now the whole deal is off. He'll tell your mother and father, and they will tell the parents of all the other kids."

I acted like I was angry, but I was really happy. I hadn't volunteered to go but this would give Tom a good excuse to not go.

"Uncle Steve gave me his word he won't tell a soul," Seth said. "I just wanted him to know because he is interested in ghosts and ghost stories."

Well, I thought to myself, if that is the case, it isn't even important enough to mention to Tom.

That night when Tom and I went up to our bedroom, I started to get undressed.

"What do you think you're doing?" Tom asked.

"Going to bed," I said.

"Oh, no, you're not," Tom said. "You are coming with me."

"You didn't hear me volunteer to go," I said as I pulled off one shoe.

"I'll need you as a witness in case the other kids back out," Tom said.

124

"Then take Sweyn as a witness," I said as I took off my other shoe.

A slow smile came to Tom's lips which suddenly broke into a big grin. "Why not?" he asked. "I'll take you both, if big brother isn't afraid."

I put my shoes back on trying to think of some excuse for not going. Maybe I could pretend I was suddenly very sick. No, Tom was too smart for that. And if I said I was afraid to go, that would make me a coward. I was trapped.

We had to wait until almost nine o'clock before Sweyn came upstairs. Papa and Mamma said he was old enough to stay up an hour later than Tom and me. Tom met him at the top of the stairs and brought him into our bedroom.

"We are going to Silverlode as soon as the curfew whistle blows," Tom said. "I'm going to prove there is no such thing as a ghost."

"You must be crazy," Sweyn said and looked afraid.

"I'm not crazy," Tom said, "but it looks as if us little grade-school kids have more courage than you big Academy fellows."

Sweyn had to admit he was a coward or go after that. Tom removed the screen from our bedroom window and we all shinnied down the elm tree. We went to our corral and waited in the bright moonlight. Parley was the first to arrive, then Sammy and Danny, followed by Seth. A few minutes later Basil arrived.

We all sneaked up alleys until we came to the town limits and the sign. We walked along the old road until we were at the corner of Whiskey Row, which used to be the main street of the mining camp, and Corry Street.

I looked around and began to shiver. The thrifty Mormons had torn down many of the wooden buildings to use the

125

lumber for making barns and pens, but there were still several deserted buildings on Whiskey Row. And I could see old weather-beaten shacks on both sides of the canyon, and the entrance to several old mine tunnels, and the giant excavations of big mines now overgrown with weeds and underbrush.

Tom led us up Corry Street as if he was just taking us on a nice safe hike. We had only gone a few steps when we heard a ghostly sound and all of us except Tom stopped. He looked back over his shoulder.

"It was just an owl," he said.

We continued on to the end of Corry Street and started up a trail that led to Boot Hill.

"Go single file now," Tom ordered us. "We are safe as long as we stay on the path. Get off it and you might fall into an old mine shaft or tunnel or an old well."

We were about halfway up the path leading to the cemetery when we heard a roaring flapping sound and saw what looked like a thousand bats flying out of a hole by the side of the path. That was enough to make even Tom stop.

Seth was the first to speak. "May-may-maybe they are vampire bats," he said, stuttering he was so scared. "My Uncle Steve said vampire bats will attack a person and drink their blood."

"These are mine bats," Tom said. "You don't see them attacking us, do you? Come on."

Tom continued to lead us up the trail until we came to a place where the ground leveled out and we could see Boot Hill. In the eerie moonlight I could see old weather-beaten wooden grave markers and two big marble headstones almost as high as I was. I knew one of those marble headstones was

126

over the grave of Mr. Tinker because Papa had showed it to us on our daylight trip to Silverlode.

"Take a good look, fellows," Tom said casually. You'd think he'd told us to look at a nice flower garden. "You don't see any ghost, do you? I told you there was no such thing as a ghost."

He had no sooner got the words out of his mouth when the ghost of Tinker came right up out of its grave behind its headstone. He was dressed in a white sheet just like a ghost is supposed to be.

"*Ohhhhhhh!*" the ghost cried out in a shrill high voice. "It is so cold and dark in that grave."

Then he saw us and the most shrill and terrifying cackling laughter came from him I'd ever heard.

My feet felt as if they were nailed to the ground and my tongue suddenly got so big I couldn't even scream. I could feel the hair on my head standing as stiff as bristles on a hairbrush. I could hear all the other kids except Tom screaming with terror. They all took off, running lickity-split down the trail.

Tom grabbed my arm and spun me around as the ghost started coming toward us. "Let's get out of here!" he shouted as he gave me a push.

My feet came loose from the ground, and my tongue got small again. I let out a terrified scream and ran like sixty down the trail with Tom behind me and the sound of that crazy, horrible, cackling laughter of the ghost in my ears.

By the time Tom and I reached the corner of Corry Street and turned onto Whiskey Row, the other kids were a block in front of us. And who do you think was in the lead? My big brother Sweyn!

I took out after them, and if I'd ever run that fast at the

127

foot races at the County Fair, I'd have won every prize. I thought the other kids would wait for us when they reached the town limits of Adenville, but they didn't. I learned the next day none of them stopped until they were safe in their own beds.

When Tom and I climbed through our bedroom window, my oldest brother was sitting on my bed puffing like a racehorse. Tom and I sat down beside him, and boy, were we puffing too. I never thought I could run more than a mile at top speed, but I did that night.

Sweyn was the first to get his breath. "I hope your great brain doesn't get any more crazy ideas," he whispered so Mamma, Papa, and Aunt Bertha wouldn't hear us downstairs. "And don't ever try to tell me again there is no ghost of Silverlode."

"My great brain still tells me there is no such thing as a ghost," Tom whispered.

"Then your great brain has shrunk down to the size of a pea," Sweyn said. "We saw the ghost come right up out of its grave, and we heard the ghost. What more do you want? And I didn't see you standing there and telling the ghost there was no such thing as a ghost."

"At least I wasn't leading the pack like you," Tom said. "I made sure J.D. got out of there because I knew he was plenty scared."

"And you weren't," Sweyn said sarcastically.

"Why should I have been?" Tom asked. "Did you ever hear of a ghost who physically harmed anybody?"

"Then why did you run?" Sweyn asked.

"Because my big Academy brother ran like a scared rabbit and left J.D. standing there petrified with fright," Tom said.

128

Sweyn got up from the bed. "Just count me out of any more crazy ideas you get," he said. "I'm going to bed."

Tom and I got undressed and into bed. Then a reaction set in on me. I began to shiver and whimper with fright.

"Go to sleep," Tom said.

"How can I?" I asked. "That ghost is going to haunt us for sure for disturbing him. I don't care what your great brain tells you. For my money that was an honest-to-goodness ghost."

"Maybe it was and maybe it wasn't," Tom said. "If it was a ghost, my great brain won't rest until I get a chance to talk to it and find out what makes a ghost, and why they go around haunting places and people. And if it isn't a real ghost, my great brain won't rest until I find out who has been scaring the daylights out of kids and grownups all these years."

"Well, all I can say is that you're not going to get any help from me," I said.

When I woke up in the morning, I was more sure than ever that Tom wouldn't get any help from me. I had nothing but terrible nightmares all night with ghosts chasing me.

After we'd finished our morning chores, Tom went up to his loft to think. This was one time I hoped his great brain had sense enough to tell him to leave ghosts alone.

That afternoon we went swimming. Parley, Sammy, Danny, Seth, and Basil went with us. They all looked red-eyed as if they'd had the same kind of nightmares I'd had. We talked about the ghost on our way to the swimming hole. Everybody agreed it was a sure-enough ghost except Tom.

"My great brain won't rest until I find out if it was a real ghost," Tom said.

Basil shook his head. "If you don't find out last night, you never do."

"And," I said, "your great brain is never going to get any rest as far as I'm concerned."

The others nodded in agreement.

"All I want you to do is to go to Silverlode with me again tonight," Tom said. "If we see and hear the ghost again, then I'll believe in ghosts. But maybe we all just imagined we saw and heard a ghost last night. How about it?"

This time Tom didn't get one volunteer.

"Are you cowards or men?" Tom demanded. "I say anybody who refuses to go is a coward."

Tom had us over a barrel.

"I'll go." Parley was the first to volunteer.

The rest of us had to admit we were cowards or meet Tom outside our barn that night.

Well, I sure wouldn't have volunteered if I'd known what Tom planned to do that night. I would have cheerfully let every kid in town call me a coward first. But I didn't know until we went up to our room that night.

"I didn't want to tell the other kids, J.D.," Tom said as we waited for the curfew whistle to blow, "but tonight I'm going to capture that ghost or whatever it is. And you are going to help me."

"Oh, no, I'm not," I said. "The ghost of Silverlode never did me any harm and won't as long as I leave him alone."

"Oh, yes, you are," Tom said.

"What are you going to do with a ghost if you do capture it?" I asked, hoping that would make him change his mind.

"If it is a real ghost," Tom said, "I'll interview it. I'll find out all about ghosts and Papa can print the story in the *Advocate*. It will make him world-famous. You wouldn't do anything to prevent Papa from becoming a world-famous journalist would you?"

131

"Of course not," I answered.

"That is why I knew you would help me," Tom said. "And if it isn't a real ghost like my great brain tells me, I'll find out who has been scaring kids and grownups by pretending to be a ghost."

The curfew whistle finally blew. We met the other kids in front of our barn. Tom went into the barn, where I'd locked up my dogs. When he came out, he was carrying Sweyn's lariat.

Sammy pointed at it. "Why the lariat?" he asked.

"I'll tell you when we get there," Tom said.

Again we sneaked without being seen to the town limits and then walked to the corner of Whiskey Row and Corry Streets.

"Now I'll tell you fellows about the lariat," Tom said. "I'm going to capture that ghost or whatever it is tonight. You fellows stay here for five minutes. That will give J.D. and me time to sneak up that other trail leading to a mine in back of the cemetery. I'm going to sneak up behind the ghost or whatever it is when he steps in front of the tombstone and lasso him to the tombstone."

"Not me," Seth said. "I'm going home right now."

"You have nothing to be afraid of," Tom said. "If the ghost is going to be mad at anybody it will be J.D. and me for trying to capture him and not you fellows."

"How will we know when it is five minutes?" Sammy asked.

"All you've got to do is count slowly up to three hundred," Tom said. "Then go up the trail to where we were last night. Stay there until the ghost appears and stands up in front of that big tombstone. Then you can all beat it home.

132

That is, unless you want to stay and help me capture the ghost."

Tom sure didn't get any volunteers that time.

"J.D. and I will leave now, so you can start counting," Tom said.

I had no choice but to follow my brother or be branded a coward. I knew Papa would rather see me dead than walking around a coward. And I was sure I was going to drop dead from fright if nothing else that night.

Tom ran with me down Whiskey Row to another street, where we turned to the right. We ran softly to the end of that street and then began to walk carefully and quietly up a trail that led to a mine in back of Boot Hill. Then we crawled on our hands and knees through the cemetery until we came to the big marble tombstone in back of the big tombstone of Mr. Tinker's grave. We were only about thirty feet from where we'd seen the ghost the night before. Tom peeked around the tombstone where we were hiding.

"There is something fishy about this," he whispered to me. "The ghost or whatever it is is hiding behind the Tinker tombstone."

My curiosity overcame my fright. I peeked around the headstone. Sure enough, I could see something white crouched behind the tombstone in front of us.

Then we heard the footsteps of the kids coming up the trail to Boot Hill. Again I peeked around the tombstone. I saw them stop where we had all stopped the night before. Then the ghost got up from behind the headstone and stepped around in front of it with his back toward us, facing the other kids.

"*Ohhhhhh!*" the ghost cried in that high shrill voice of his. "It is so cold and dark in that grave." Then he began that terrible cackling laughter that sent chills all over my body. I stared with fascinated horror as Tom got up and walked toward the ghost. He stopped about fifteen feet from the ghost and made a loop in the lariat. The kids began to scream with terror and run down the trail. Tom began to whirl the lariat over his head. It made a whining noise which the ghost couldn't hear because of his cackling laughter and the screaming of the kids. Then Tom made a perfect throw with the lariat. The noose dropped smack over the ghost and the big tombstone. Tom jerked it tight and then began running around the big tombstone and the ghost, making coil after coil of rope, tying the ghost to the tombstone. When the end of the lariat got short, Tom stopped behind the tombstone and tied it with a slipknot to the noose of the lariat.

The ghost wasn't cackling that crazy laughter anymore. He was hogtied to that tombstone like a calf at a rodeo.

Tom motioned for me to follow him as he ran down the trail toward Corry Street. I sure didn't need any encouragement.

I guess the ghost was so surprised he couldn't think of anything to say until then.

"Come back and let me go!" I heard him shouting. "I won't hurt you!"

Tom and I didn't stop until we reached Whiskey Row. "I got him tied so he can't get away," he said puffing. "You go get Papa and Uncle Mark. I'll wait here."

I tried to speak but couldn't for a moment. I was so chilled with fright I felt as if I was in a bathtub filled with ice.

"I thought you were going to interview the ghost," I finally managed to say and my voice sounded as if it was far away.

134

"I decided to let Papa do that if it is a real ghost," Tom said. "Now go get him and Uncle Mark."

I didn't stop running until I flung open the front door of our house and entered the parlor, where Papa, Mamma, and Aunt Bertha were sitting. They all stood up at the same time and stared at me as if I'd popped right up out of the floor.

"What are you doing out of bed?" Mamma demanded.

Papa looked at the dirt and cockleburs sticking to my Levi britches and shirt. "And where in the name of Jupiter have you been?" he asked.

I tried to talk but couldn't because my breath was like fire coming out of my lungs.

Papa began to pound me on the back to try and help me catch my breath. Mamma ran into the kitchen and came back with a glass of water. With Papa pounding my back and Mamma getting some water down my throat, at last I could talk.

"T.D. has captured the ghost of Silverlode!" I cried. "He has the ghost tied to a tombstone in Boot Hill and wants you to come interview it, and bring Uncle Mark!"

Papa looked at me as if I was a ghost. He stood there stunned. Then he held out his hands in a pleading gesture toward Mamma. "Why, oh, why did you have to give birth to a son who hasn't given us a moment's peace since the day he was born?"

Mamma ignored the question and acted quickly, as she always did in a crisis. She went to the telephone and called the Allies Saloon. Uncle Mark wasn't there so she called the other saloon and got him on the phone. She told him to come at once and to bring a couple of horses.

Papa and I were waiting at our front gate when Uncle Mark rode up riding a strange horse and leading another one.

"Tena said it was urgent," he said. "I borrowed these horses from a couple of cowboys. What is this all about?"

"You will never believe it," Papa said as he mounted the extra horse. Uncle Mark held out his hand and lifted me up behind him.

"T.D. has got the ghost of Silverlode tied to a tombstone in Boot Hill," I shouted at Uncle Mark. "Let's hurry before the ghost gets loose."

Uncle Mark didn't waste any more words. We galloped off toward Silverlode.

Tom was waiting at the corner of Whiskey Row and Corry Street for us.

"Did the ghost get away?" I asked as I slipped off the rump of the horse.

"No," Tom said. "I walked up the trail just a minute or so ago and he is still tied to the tombstone."

Papa and Uncle Mark dismounted, with Papa glaring at Tom. "I'll deal with you later," Papa said.

"My great brain did it," Tom said proudly. "If it is a real ghost, you can interview it and that will make you a famous journalist." Then Tom shook his head. "But my great brain keeps telling me there is no such thing as a ghost. That is why I sent for you and Uncle Mark, so you could lock up in jail whoever it is that has been scaring kids and grownups with this ghost business."

Then we walked to the end of Corry Street and started up the trail to Boot Hill.

"I wonder who the poor fool is," Uncle Mark said and surprised me by laughing. "It would serve him right if we left him there until morning."

"It is the ghost of Mr. Tinker," I said. "He came up from the grave just like he did last night."

136

"Last night?" Papa asked. "It gets worse and worse."

We came to the end of the trail to where we could plainly see the ghost tied to the tombstone.

"I assure you, John," Uncle Mark said, "that it isn't the ghost of Mr. Tinker."

The ghost must have heard us. "Whoever you are get me out of this," he shouted.

Uncle Mark began to laugh softly as we walked to the tombstone. He was still laughing as he untied the lariat.

"Let's see what we've got here," Uncle Mark said as he lifted the sheet off the ghost. "As I live and breathe if it isn't Steve Smith, the old ghost-story teller himself, caught in his own trap."

And sure enough, there was Seth's uncle looking as if he wished he really was a ghost and could disappear.

"I was only trying to help," he said. Then he got angry. "You were one of those who encouraged this ghost of Silverlode business."

"Guilty," Uncle Mark said. "But I only did it to make sure the kids in town don't dare come here and end up like the Knudson and Bartell boy. I didn't come here and run around this cemetery with a sheet on."

"I had to do it," Steve Smith said. "Yesterday my nephew told me that he and some other boys were coming here after curfew last night. I figured I'd give them such a scare that he would never come here again. Well, I did give all those kids such a scare last night by pretending to be a ghost I didn't think any of them would ever dare set foot in this ghost town again."

"That is understandable," Uncle Mark said sympathetically.

"But when my nephew told me after supper tonight that

one boy still wasn't convinced there was a ghost, and they were coming here again tonight," Steve Smith said, "I thought if I pretended to be the ghost of Silverlode one more time, it would convince even this boy there was a ghost."

Then he looked at Papa as if he wanted to take a punch at my father. "But that son of yours wasn't satisfied to see and hear a ghost two nights in a row. He had to capture a ghost."

"I'm sorry, Mr. Smith," Tom said, "but my great brain wouldn't rest until I found out if there were really ghosts or not. If it was real, I wanted to interview it and find out all about ghosts so my father could print the story in the *Advocate*, and it would make him famous. And if the ghost was a fake, I wanted to prove to the other kids that there was no such thing as a ghost."

"I'm glad I don't live in Adenville," Mr. Smith said. "When this story gets out, I doubt if I'll ever even come here to visit my brother and his family again."

"Nobody will ever know except us," Uncle Mark said. "If the story got out, every kid in Adenville would start making this ghost town a playground, and that could lead to another tragedy."

Then Uncle Mark put his hand on Tom's shoulder. "You and John are going to tell a hair-raising tale of what happened here tonight. You are going to say when you tried to lasso the ghost, the lariat went right through him. You are going to say the ghost caught you both and threatened to take you back into his grave with him if you ever set foot in Silverlode again."

"But that would be lying, Uncle Mark," Tom said. "And besides, I'd have to admit my great brain was wrong, and there really are ghosts."

138

Papa had been standing with his cheeks so blown up I thought he'd take off like a balloon.

"You and J.D. will do exactly as your Uncle Mark says," Papa said. "This ghost town must be strictly off limits to every boy in Adenville. Now give me your word as a Fitzgerald that you both will do as your uncle has suggested."

Tom sure looked disappointed. "All right, Papa," he said. "Word of honor."

"Me too," I said.

Uncle Mark looked at Seth's uncle. "I suppose you came on a horse," he said.

"I hid it in back of the old Miners Hotel," Steve Smith said. "And thanks, Marshal, for keeping this story a secret."

I rode behind Papa and Tom behind Uncle Mark until we stopped in front of our house. We slid off over the rumps of the horses. Papa dismounted and handed the reins of the horse to Uncle Mark. Then my uncle looked down at Tom.

"I will sort of hate seeing you leave for Salt Lake City in a couple of weeks," he said. Then he rode down Main Street laughing as if he'd just told a very funny joke.

Mamma and Aunt Bertha began hugging Tom and making a fuss over him when we entered the parlor. I was as much a part of the adventure as my brother, but they just ignored me. Papa walked to his rocking chair and slumped down in it. He put his head between his hands and his head began swaying back and forth as if he had a terrible headache. Finally he looked up at Tom.

"I don't know what I'm going to do with you," he said.

"The boys are safe," Mamma said, "and let us thank their guardian angels for that."

"We have one son who is absolutely deaf in his left ear," Papa said, as he pointed at Tom.

139

"What makes you say a silly thing like that?" Mamma asked.

"Every boy is born with a guardian angel on his left shoulder," Papa said. "And that guardian angel whispers into the boy's ear every time that boy does something wrong or even thinks about doing something wrong. That is why I say that T.D. is stone deaf in his left ear. He hasn't heard one word his guardian angel whispered in his ear since the day he was born."

Papa could sure exaggerate at times.

"I can't help it," Tom said, "that I was born with a great brain that has to know everything. I just had to find out if there was such a thing as a real ghost."

"Then why in the name of Jupiter didn't you just ask me?" Papa demanded.

"I did ask you a long time ago," Tom said. "And you led me to believe there was a ghost of Silverlode."

"I think he has you there, my dear," Mamma said with that sort of half smile on her face she always got when teasing Papa.

"That is right!" Papa cried as if being persecuted. "Put all the blame on me. If we had woke up tomorrow morning and found our two sons missing and their bodies had never been found like the Knudson and Bartell boys, you would be the first to blame me for not telling them there was a ghost of Silverlode to scare them away from the place."

Tom's great brain must have been working like sixty to try and get us out of being punished. "If you'd told me the truth," he said as if everything was Papa's fault, "I'd have kept the secret from the other kids."

"It is very late," Mamma said, putting an end to the argument. "You boys go to bed. We will discuss it further in the morning."

Papa stared at Tom as if saying a prayer. "And please stay in bed until morning," he pleaded.

The next morning Papa kept us in suspense until we had finished eating breakfast and he was having a second cup of coffee.

"Your mother and I have talked things over," he said. Then he looked straight at Tom. "You and S.D. will be leaving for the Academy in Salt Lake City in two weeks. We all want to be as close as a family should be during that time. There will be no punishment."

Then Papa looked at Tom with an appealing look in his eyes like a hungry dog begging for a bone. "Do you think it possible, T.D., for you and your great brain to give your mother and me and the rest of this town a breathing spell for just two weeks?"

"I think so," Tom said.

Papa lost his temper and slammed his fist down so hard on the table it shook the dishes on it. "I want you to do more than just think about it!" he said.

"All right, Papa, I promise," Tom said.

Tom kept his word to Uncle Mark and Papa. He told such a hair-raising tale about the ghost of Silverlode that you couldn't have got any kid in town to pass that sign on the road to Silverlode for all the gumdrops in the Z.C.M.I. store.

He also kept his word to Papa by giving his great brain a rest and doing everything he could to please Papa, Mamma, and Aunt Bertha. And, I guess, because his great brain was resting and not working in its usual style, he got very gener-

141

ous with me. He told me the day before he was to leave for Salt Lake City with Sweyn that he would let me use his bike for just ten cents a week.

"You can afford it, J.D.," he said as we sat on our back porch making the deal. "I've talked to Papa, and he admits it is only fair to raise your allowance to twenty cents a week because you will be doing all the chores."

It was the best deal I'd ever made with Tom and it gave me an idea. I wasn't the smartest fellow around, but I'd been swindled so many times by the Great Brain that I knew all the angles. That was one advantage of being the victim of a swindle. It taught a fellow how to make other kids the victims. I knew plenty of kids in town who didn't own a bike who would gladly pay me five cents a day to use Tom's bicycle.

And why should a smart kid like me, who knew all the angles now, do my own chores? The Jensen family were very poor. I could get Frank or Allan to do all my chores for ten cents a week, which would leave me a neat profit of a dime a week. It would be me and not Tom sitting on the corral fence watching somebody else do the chores.

And look at all the things I'd learned from Tom about trading and swapping things. Enough of my brother's great brain had rubbed off on me. There wasn't anything any kid in town had that I couldn't get. The thought didn't bother my conscience a bit. Somebody had to take my brother's place in Adenville, and it might as well be me. There wasn't a doubt in my mind that I'd soon be the richest kid in town.